"A compelling war novel in the traditio          ⌐ Brien. Mark B. Arrieta wrote this book for his family so they would know of their heritage. As a result, we readers have been blessed with a story marked by tragedy and the miracle of a Basque family's resilience."

—Hank Nuwer, author of *Sons of the Dawn: A Basque Odyssey*

"Though *Son of a Basque* is offered as fiction, this terrific, moving, and thoroughly engaging book shares an important piece of history that I hadn't yet discovered and gave me a new perspective on the immigrant experience. I loved it."

—Gigi Levangie, *New York Times* bestselling author of seven novels, including *The Starter Wife* and *Maneater*

"The science of epigenetics has proven beyond a shadow of a doubt that the fears, beliefs, and subsequent behaviors of our ancestors are passed on to the genes of their offspring. In this amazing memoir masquerading as a novel, *Son of a Basque* reveals why learning about our parents' and grandparents' past struggles is an essential element in understanding our own present-day difficulties."

—Joseph McClendon III, peak-performance coach and author of *Dare to Be Magnificent*

"*Son of a Basque* does a touching and engaging job of bringing the human side to history. The perspective on 'hard times' was a welcome reminder as I learned about the Basque people."

—Misti Wriston, author of *Here Comes the Sun: Step Up, Shine Your Light, and Share Your Brilliance*

"*Son of a Basque* is a fascinating read and points up the emotional crisis we have with different generations trying to find common ground. For anyone who wants to understand the emotional trauma that many immigrants and families go through, this is a must-read."

—Larry Namer, founder of E! Entertainment Television

"A thought-provoking novel, *Son of a Basque* shows us that the hardships and trauma immigrants suffer—even if they seemingly overcome them—can leave a mark on future generations. Knowing that the story is based on the author's life makes it even more fascinating."

—Siri Lindley, world champion triathlete and author of *Surfacing: From the Depths of Self-Doubt to Winning Big and Living Fearlessly*

"*Son of a Basque* captures the quintessential American Story, set against an epic canvas of Dust Bowl poverty, world war, and the 1940s prison system. To follow Mark Vergara on the journey of his life is to witness the son of an immigrant generation discover the meaning in hardship, loss, love, family, and his own sense of what defines a man."

—John Capone, award-winning filmmaker and director of *Neon Bleed*

"Part novel, part memoir, *Son of a Basque* is sometimes heartbreaking, sometimes funny, and always entertaining. I was engrossed from the first page. We have much to learn from the struggles of our ancestors."

—Dorothy Lucey, adjunct professor and television personality

"This story opened my eyes to the greatness that exists in the ordinary. It is about a man who does not let the hardships of his youth determine the person he chooses to be. *Son of a Basque* is an inspirational read that will tug at your heart."

—J. L. Witterick, international bestselling author

"Deborah Driggs does a remarkable job of reviving the story of her grandfather Mark Arrieta, whose bare survival and ultimate success was penned by him before his passing in the late '90s. This book should remind all of us that those before us endured great hardship and pain so our lives could be better. Incredible storytelling."

—Suzanne Takowsky, Publisher, *Beverly Hills Times* magazine, and author of the forthcoming *Every Woman's Life*

"*Son of a Basque* is an incredible story built on courage, perseverance, and the incredible power of the human spirit. This story humbles the generations of today with the remarkable path created by our ancestors so we could live the life we have. I am in complete awe of the profound strength of this family and Mark B. Arrieta for documenting his family's legacy and bringing this wisdom forward. Every human young and old needs to read this inspirational story. Absolutely amazing!"

—Lauren Magers, founder of NPRP Media and creator of the Happy Life System

"*Son of a Basque* weaves an intricate personal story into an historical context with a narrator who is completely authentic. If there were more books like it, we would more likely relate to the challenges of those who arrived on this shore and the power of each generational decision that followed."

—Cheryl R. Oliver, author, poet, and writing coach

"A thought-provoking novel, *Son of a Basque* illustrates for people who haven't had this kind of experience the hardships and trauma immigrants suffer and how they can affect future generations. Intergenerational traumatic family patterns are important to understand."

—Chris M. King, executive performance coach, speaker, and author of *Renegotiate Your Existence: Unlock Your Impossible Life*

"This is a straightforward rendering of a life lived and, typical of those from 'the greatest generation,' utterly without sentimentality or aggrandizement. Harrowing stories of World War II and the Vietnam conflict are punctuated by unvarnished tales of working in the depraved hell that was the San Quentin penitentiary. But love and family are also given their due. Although rarely spoken of with such unselfconscious candor, this is what much of actual life on earth has been like, unsentimental, pragmatic, and just plain tough."

—D. W. Brown, writer, director, and acting instructor

"This is the most moving and inspiring story. A must-read for every person who has gone through or is going through any transition in life or trauma. It is a story of love and resilience that will touch your heart and soul. A true lesson that through all challenges we can persevere and create greatness."

—Kim Zoller, founder and CEO, ID360, and coauthor of *You Did What?, You Said What?*, and *Enhancing Your Executive Edge*

"I thoroughly enjoyed reading *Son of a Basque*; there is so much living history in the book. The story reminded me of my father who also emigrated to this country in search of a better life."

—Sheila Mac, reboot strategist and host of *The Sheila Mac Show*

# SON OF A BASQUE

# SON OF A BASQUE

## MARK B. ARRIETA

### DEBORAH DRIGGS

Crystal Woods Publishing

Crystal Woods Publishing
www.crystalwoodspublishing.com

ORDERING INFORMATION
**Quantity sales:** Special discounts are available on quantity purchases by corporations, associations, and others. For details, please contact the "Special Sales Department" at the above address.
**Orders by US trade bookstores and wholesalers.** Please contact BCH: (800) 431-1579 or visit www.bookch.com for details.

Cataloging-in-Publication data

Names: Arrieta, Mark B., author. | Driggs, Deborah, author.
Title: Son of a Basque / Mark B. Arrieta [and Deborah Driggs.]
Description: Los Angeles, CA: Crystal Woods Publisher, 2022.
Identifiers: LCCN: 2022913545 | ISBN: 978-1-955862-04-2
Subjects: LCSH Basque Americans—Fiction. | Immigrants—United States—
    Fiction. | Soldiers—United
States—Fiction. | World War, 1939-1945—Fiction. | Historical fiction. | BISAC
    FICTION / Historical /
General | FICTION / Biographical
Classification: LCC PS3601 .R75 2022 | DDC 813.6—dc23

Printed in the United States of America
26 25 24 23 22     10 9 8 7 6 5 4 3 2 1

# A NOTE TO THE READER

More than forty years ago, my father asked me for assistance in typing his book. I was only too happy to help. Since he had never been the type of dad who sat his children on his knee and told them stories about growing up, his words captured my curiosity. As I grew older, I often wondered about what my parents had to endure and what it was like being raised in another time and place. It was indeed a treat to learn about the man I knew as my father.

The story in this book spans many decades, beginning in the early 1900s. Combining truth and fiction always leaves one to wonder what is real and what is not. Most of what you will read is true. However, the names of some of the places mentioned were changed because they no longer exist today, and certain people were fictionalized because of privacy concerns. Some editors asked if the stories about what occurred in the prison were really true. I can only say that truth is indeed stranger than fiction—and often scarier.

I was raised as an Air Force brat. My dad spent his entire life in the military. At just eighteen years old he did not hesitate to sign up for active duty following the Pearl Harbor attack. Selflessly, he left his mother, sisters, and brothers and put everything on hold, including his own dreams.

He found himself fighting for others' freedom on foreign soil. Without his sacrifice, their cause would have been lost. But he carried onward, no matter the cost, and endured many horrors.

He was haunted by the faces of his brothers-in-arms who fell all around. After those who survived returned home, some were left with memories to face all alone, while others found themselves in the company of friends and family. Those who survived were forever scarred emotionally and physically.

Dad was a clever man but was never afraid of having a laugh at his own expense. He was hardworking, compassionate toward everyone, and deserving of the success and rich life he enjoyed. He was also very proud of his Basque heritage.

My father passed in 1998, and his book seemed to have been lost; however, when my mother passed in 2017, my daughter and I found the manuscript pages in a storage box. They were still in good enough shape for us to piece together the story for publication. It has been our one and only project for the past few years.

It has been said that you never really know someone until they pass into the next life. My father's story has taught me so much.

I'd like to share some of the quotes my father loved dearly, which reveal his character:

We are determined that before the sun sets on this terrible struggle our flag will be recognized throughout the world as a symbol of freedom on the one hand and of overwhelming power on the other.
—George C. Marshall, US Army Chief of Staff

To have the United States at our side was to me the greatest joy. . . . Now at this very moment I knew the United States was in the war, up to the neck and in to the death. So, we had won after all! . . . Hitler's fate was sealed. Mussolini's fate was sealed. As for the Japanese, they would be ground to powder.
—Prime Minister Winston Churchill (after the Japanese attack on Pearl Harbor)

It is foolish and wrong to mourn the men who died. Rather, we should thank God that such men lived.
—General George S. Patton Jr.

Dorothy Arrieta Stangle

# CHAPTER ONE

"HEY, LITTLE MAN," they would shout at me. "Where are your sisters? Go back inside and tell your sweet pussy sisters we'll be waiting for them in one of those empty rooms upstairs. Did you hear us, Vergara?"

Of course I heard them. Every day as I came out of that stinking hellhole known as the Lincoln Rooms I heard them, but I pretended not to.

One of the men grabbed me by the right arm and gave me a swift kick in the shinbone, but I raised my leg and stuck my knee right into his crotch as hard as I could. I stared at him, speechless, backing away from the tight little knot of men before they could slice me with their knives. I ran away as fast as I could, until I was out of breath and fell against the side of a tree, panting and cursing the day I was born.

"Why did you have to die, Pappa?" I said to the tree, to the air around me, and to the great sky above, which never answered.

"I need you now, Pappa, more than I ever needed you before. Where are you? Why did you have to leave us like this?"

I expected an answer from him. I wanted it so badly that I was angry when it didn't come and more confused about life than I'd ever been. My father was real to me, even though his bones were in the ground. I would pray so hard for him to come and help me, but he never came. Nobody ever came to help the Vergaras.

The year was 1928, the worst year I have ever known in my life. I was only a child then, almost ten years old, but even if I had been a

1

man, it would still have been difficult to accept the shadow of death that lurked over my family.

It was easier for me than it was for my mother, since all I knew about death was what she had told me. "Your soul goes up to Heaven and rests for eternity with God." But I didn't know who God was, or what the word *eternity* meant. They were only words, without feelings, without understanding.

My mother must have known. She must have known that spending the rest of her life with only memories of death and deprivation would seem like an eternity.

We lived in Big Bend, Colorado, where I was born. At that time, my father was almost sixty years old. Everybody called him Vergara the Basque.

My father worked on a large dairy farm, which entailed not only milking but also the cultivating of feed for the large herd of cows and other stock. He was never able to take a day off and had been milking the cows twice a day, seven days a week, for four years.

Although he never complained, the hard work was beginning to show on his face and in his heart. When he became sick, we thought at first that all he needed was a good long rest, but one day he was unable to get up in the morning and had to be rushed to the county hospital, where they found he had cancer of the pancreas and colon.

It has always been hard for a proud man to accept his own weakness, his own mortality, and for my father, it was a blow like a thunderbolt.

Being the oldest boy, I was allowed to go with my mother to visit him. All he would say was, "I'm sorry for letting you down this way, so sorry for being a failure, Aurora."

"But it's not your fault, Miguel," my mother quietly answered.

"We'll get along all right, Pappa. We'll take care of Mamma. Don't you worry."

This made him sit up on his elbow and shout at me. "I'm not dead yet, young man! So, don't put me in the grave, and don't weep for me, not yet, understand?"

"But I only meant that . . ."

"I know exactly what you meant," he said, lying back down again and wiping his forehead with the palm of his hand.

"He only meant that we are fine, Miguel," my mother quickly said, trying to make us both feel better. "And we miss you very much. We are praying for you to get better, every morning and every night, Miguel."

"That's all I meant, Pappa." I went up to kiss him, but he turned his face away and sighed deeply.

"I will fight this thing," he quickly said, not allowing me to kiss his face. "And I will win, Aurora. I will win this fight in the end, you'll see."

While he was recuperating in the hospital, it was clear to the dairy owner that my father could no longer work for him. He finally told my mother he would have to replace him and eventually we would have to move.

My parents knew a man who owned some property in Lamar, Colorado, sixteen miles south of Big Bend. This man had agreed to let us live in one of the houses on his farm, rent-free for a year, until my father was strong enough to return to work.

With the help of friends and the loan of a wagon from the dairy owner, Mr. Froman, we moved our belongings into the house, and my mother began looking for a job.

I already had a younger brother, Carlos; two older sisters, Delores and Susanna; and two younger sisters, Conchita and Rosalie. My mother was now pregnant with her seventh child, although she never admitted it to Mrs. Craig, her new employer.

Mrs. Craig was an extremely wealthy widow, and it was fortunate for all of us that she allowed my mother to work for her, since we now had enough money to buy clothes, enabling me and Carlos and our older sisters to go to school.

Our good fortune didn't last long. We had to move again, and now all the children had to help out, even the little ones. I guess we were lucky to find work, since hundreds of people were already going hungry and begging for jobs and bread. But we children didn't feel lucky, having to work in the sugar beet fields all day.

We all felt like we were living like gypsies in those days, since we had to move again, this time to a small community called Granada, in the eastern part of Colorado close to the Kansas border.

When he got better, father met some Basque people there who were sheep owners and was offered a job looking after three thousand head of sheep. Carlos and I would visit him once a week, riding our horses to his camp, and everything seemed normal and happy again.

We should have known better, but we were so young and full of hope. One day they brought my father home from the sheep ranch, and we knew his days were numbered, but we never knew tragedy was also unexpected.

On the eighth of July, my youngest brother was born, and I have never been able to forget it, since it was also the day that death came into our house.

I began to think about death and what my life would be like when my father was gone. I never thought about my own death or that of my brothers or sisters, for we were young children, not old and sick as my father was. But I learned the day that my youngest brother was born that we all face the fate of death, even children.

That particular morning, little Rosalie came up to me after she had finished her prayers. Putting her hand in mine, she said, "Do you think the new baby will be a boy or a girl, Mark?"

"I hope it's a boy," I told her, "so that Carlos and I can teach him how to ride and fish."

"Well, I hope it's a girl," Rosalie answered, "so that I can teach her how to cook and sew."

"You don't know how to cook or sew," I said, laughing and dusting the top of her head with my hand.

"Well, it's just pretend," she shyly answered, "but I can pretend better than Delores or Susanna, and better than Concha! After all, I am five years old now."

Five years old, and so full of life. That was our little Rosalie. She was the prettiest one of the four girls, with large brown eyes that seemed to look at you all the time and dimpled cheeks nestled under her high cheekbones. She was a true beauty, and I loved her.

By the time my father, my two older sisters, Carlos, and I reached the beet fields that morning, my mother was already in labor. She asked Rosalie and Concha to go get the neighbors. The two little girls raced each other out the door to see who could get there first, shouting on the way that their mother was having a baby. Heads popped out of the windows all along the street, and three women with white sheets in their arms followed my sisters home.

They told my sisters to stay outside and play, but Rosalie wondered what all the white sheets were for.

"We will make one of them into a rope for your mother to hang on to until the baby is born," one of the women told her. "The others are to be used for diapers for the baby, you see, little one?"

"Oh, diapers!" said Rosalie. "Yes, I see."

Rosalie snuck back inside the house, grabbed a handful of the torn sheets, and took them out to the well to wash them for the new baby.

Conchita had fallen asleep in the shade of a tree, and Rosalie was all alone when she reached over the top of the well to bring the bucket up. It must have been too far for her to reach it, and we could only assume that she had climbed up onto the shelf of the well and leaned over to grab the bucket.

As my mother cried out in pain and baby Pablo was coming into the world, Rosalie was falling down, down into the water, beating her arms and kicking her legs helplessly. Because of my mother's screams, no one heard little Rosalie's. In all the excitement of Pablo's birth, no one realized that she was missing until the three women had finished their work, placed the newborn in my mother's arms, and were leaving the house.

They saw Conchita, still sleeping under the tree, and woke her up, saying, "Go with your sister into the fields, and tell the others that they have a new baby brother. Where is your sister, anyway?"

"I don't know," the sleepy child answered, rubbing her eyes.

"Well, go and find her, quickly now, and then tell the others. All right, Concha?"

Conchita, now six years old, called out for Rosalie, running in every direction as fast as her little legs would allow her to go. She looked everywhere for Rosalie—everywhere except in the well.

"I tiptoed up to it," she later said, "and I didn't want to look inside because it was so far down to the bottom, and I couldn't even see the bottom except if the light from the sun was shining into the well. But I knew something was wrong, so I ran straight to the fields and came to find you."

She was crying hysterically when she found us and wasn't able to say anything but, "Come, Pappa. Help!" We got up from our knees, and my father shook Conchita's shoulders, but she was still unable to speak. He picked her up and started running with her in his arms, thinking that something terrible had happened to our mother. Then the rest of us followed him, running and crying before we even knew what was wrong but knowing a tragedy had occurred and fearing the worst.

When we reached our house, out of breath and trembling with fear, we ran into our mother's bedroom. She was resting peacefully with the baby at her side. My father put Conchita down and spoke to our mother.

"Where is Rosalie?" he gently asked, "and are you all right, Aurora?"

My mother looked up at him and murmured, "Yes, we have a new son, and Rosalie is playing with Conchita." Then she closed her eyes, exhausted and ready to sleep.

"But Concha came to get us," my father whispered. "Where are you, little one?" He turned to look for my sister, who had run to hide behind Susanna and was holding up the back of her skirt and sobbing into it.

"Where is your little sister, Concha?" my father asked again, trying to keep his voice under control. He took a few steps and pulled Concha out from behind Susanna's back. Then he held her face in his hands so that she would be looking at him. "Don't be afraid, little one, but simply answer me. Where do you think your sister is?"

"In the well!" Conchita shouted, beginning to cry again. "I didn't see her, but I know she's there. Oh, Pappa, I'm sorry. I'm so sorry, Pappa."

My father rushed from the house to the well. The rest of us followed as fast as we could. All except Conchita, who was now hysterical and uncontrollable. She climbed into our mother's bed, lying on the coverlet in a fetal position, grabbing hold of our mother's legs, trying to reach for comfort from her.

My father turned the handle of the well bucket without saying a word. We all waited in the deepest silence as we watched the rope moving slowly upward, dripping with water, until the empty bucket came into view. Then he put the ladder down inside the well, and I wondered who would have to climb down to the bottom, since my father was too sick to do this himself. One of our neighbors had to do the awful job of bringing my sister's body up and putting her in my father's arms.

Some of the sheets for the baby's diapers were wrapped around Rosalie, like the winding sheets used as shrouds for the dead. I could hardly bear to look at my father, holding my little sister close against his chest, so I bowed my head, as the others were doing, and asked God to please let her be alive.

Then my father shouted out, "Dear God in Heaven, help us with this child!" because Rosalie had suddenly moved. She was still alive.

My father ran with her to the house and laid her on the table in the kitchen. If only we had known what to do, we could have saved her life, but we all just stood there, looking at her dying body. She was unconscious but was trying to cough, as if to get the water out of her lungs. My father pushed her chest and raised her little arms, but he couldn't revive her. We all stood there like stones, watching her die.

My father waited until the next day to tell my mother. Her screams of anguish made us all leave the house. Only Conchita stayed with her and baby Pablo. They cried for hours; then it ceased. The first terrible fire of their grief had subsided.

We buried Rosalie, with only a stick to mark her grave, on the ninth day of July 1928. Now our mother had six children again, instead of seven.

We all knew somehow that it was time for us to move on, to pack up our belongings, sell our horse and buggy, and look for a better life somewhere else.

By the time we reached Pueblo, Colorado, we had almost run out of money, but my father had heard there was work on the western slopes of the Rockies in a farm community called Delta.

We would have to travel a great distance, from Pueblo to Salida, transferring there to a narrow-gauge railroad to get over the Monarch Pass, through Gunnison National Park, and on to Montrose. From there, we would transfer one more time and finally get to Delta.

We children had never been on a train before and had never even heard of the Rockies, so it was the beginning of a great adventure for us, even though we weren't allowed to take our old dog, Forray, along with us. We had to say good-bye to him and leave him behind with the memories of our sister Rosalie.

Before we even started the journey, as we were waiting on the platform, we heard a sound that seemed like a monster, growing louder and louder, coming closer and closer. The wooden planks under our feet started to tremble, and then we saw the monster's red eye coming straight at us. We saw the smoke it was breathing that rose in clouds around its head, and even though we wanted to pretend to be big and strong like men, Carlos and I hugged each other in fear. We were still holding on to each other when the monster finally came to a stop in front of us, breathing out its last few gasps of white-hot smoky breath.

Then we heard someone laughing at us. It was the train conductor, who had stepped onto the platform. "Don't worry," he told us, grinning from ear to ear, "I won't let it bite you."

He told us the train would be climbing up into the clouds and we would need our winter jackets ready to keep us warm. He said we might even see snow higher than the train itself. Then it was our turn to laugh, since we could hardly imagine snow being that deep. But the conductor's words turned out to be true enough when we emerged from a tunnel on the other side of a mountain, winding our way through the pass.

I don't know how any of the others in my family felt about this sight, but it made me catch my breath and hold it, as if I could make myself hold on to this beautiful vision forever.

The air turned as cold as ice, which only added to my youthful impression of being in a wonderland. When I finally exhaled again, I could see my breath stretch out in front of my mouth like a wondrous steamy mist.

My hopes were raised again. The higher we climbed into the mountains, the higher I felt my heart soaring, like a bird. I had the impression my very soul had been set free, and this was very strange to me since I had never realized how low-down I had felt before, like a bird in a cage.

When we arrived in Montrose, we made our final transfer to a regular-gauge train that would take us on the remainder of our journey, twenty-two miles to Delta. The train ran parallel to the Uncompahgre River, and the land around it was lush and green as far as the eye could see.

We arrived at the station and were surprised to see that almost everyone in town, it seemed, had come to welcome us. Since my father would be working for the Holly Sugar Corporation, their representatives had come to greet us, along with trucks and cars to move our belongings to our new home. Carlos and I rode on top of the truck so that we wouldn't miss a thing.

We were lucky enough to be given a farm with twenty acres of sugar beets to be thinned out along the banks of the Gunnison River. Carlos and I would spend many happy afternoons there, learning to fish and dreaming big dreams of becoming men.

Father was given a purchase voucher to one of the stores for buying whatever groceries and things we would all need. It didn't occur to us children that we would have to pay off these loans by doing the stoop labor of thinning out those ever-growing beet plants. The more we bought at the store, the more work we had to do. It seemed as if we would never get out of the beet fields.

Our father never told us he was dying; we children never knew that the cancer had finally begun to kill him. Only our mother knew of his agonizing pain. He was like a walking dead man without a stomach. But he worked until he couldn't stand up anymore. Then one morning he was unable to get out of bed.

Mother called the doctor, and he gave Father some pain pills to make his death more bearable, but we all knew there was little anyone could do for him now.

We were playing outside when the doctor left, shaking his head, as if to say, I can help him no more. Then our mother called us all into the house and asked us to kneel beside his bed. She was crying when she said, "Your father is dying now, and he wants to bless you all."

He made the sign of the cross and said, "I am very sorry I have to leave you now, my children. Take care of each other." And looking straight at me, he said, "Be big and strong, huh, Mark? Now is your chance to prove what a strong man you can be for the family."

"Pappa," I answered, "I will never be able to take your place, no matter how big and strong I get."

"Thank you, son," he said, looking right at me. Then he started to moan in pain. He cried out, "I don't want to die so far from home. I wish I could go back."

Mother said, "You are going back, my love, back to God."

As my father cried out in pain, my mother held him and asked, "Does it hurt so very much?"

"No, my love, my life," he answered. "I have no feeling anymore."

We children couldn't hold our sorrow anymore. We all ran outside, sobbing in one another's arms. Waiting for my father to die was like waiting for the end of the world to come. I kept hoping it wouldn't come, that maybe, if I held my breath long enough, I could save it up for him and keep him alive a little longer. But I already knew about death and how it came in its own good time.

"In God's time," as my mother said when she called us all into the house once more. "God bless him," she told us. "He isn't suffering anymore, and he died, as I always wanted him to, in my arms."

She reached over and closed his eyes, saying, "He's in God's hands now, my children."

I sat at the side of my father's bed looking at him for a long time, not fully realizing he was gone forever from my life. He looked so peaceful, with no signs at all on his face of the struggle, the fight he had waged against the cancer. It gave me a measure of strength to see him that way, because I could tell myself everything was all right for him now.

My father, Miguel Markelino Vergara, left this world at the age of fifty-nine, in September 1928.

It was a much sadder, harder world for us all when he left us.

# CHAPTER TWO

MY MOTHER was left raising six children, speaking no English, and having to pay off my father's debts to the Holly Sugar Corporation. The only way to do it was to ask for more work, filling out more cash vouchers for enough food to keep us alive during the long winter months ahead.

Taking my oldest sister with her to act as interpreter, my mother was able to get us a contract chopping sugar beets, but the winter came in late October, turning the fields wet, cold, and muddy, making it a struggle to lift the beets far enough to chop the green tops off.

We could see the snow falling miles away on the mountaintops, and we didn't see how we could survive in the adobe house with no heat or proper facilities.

Since my mother had no husband, no father for her children, we were informed by the company that we could move into a hotel in the middle of town. We jumped at the chance.

We should have stayed in our little adobe house because the hotel, known as the Lincoln Rooms, was a horrible, stinking hole of humanity. As soon as we saw the place, our hearts sank. It needed more than just a little tender loving care to make it livable; it needed to be torn down and rebuilt from scratch because it was a building unfit for human beings.

We'd never seen such poverty before, even in the simple, almost primitive houses we'd lived in. The people living there were completely ignorant. They used the toilets as garbage disposals, managing to plug up the pipes and making them utterly useless.

The electric lights in the hallways were either broken or flickering, so we always ran down the hall to our rooms, believing that something or someone was hiding in one doorway or the next. Sometimes we were right, since couples would often stand in the darkness, pressed against each other for a moment of privacy, clinging to each other in the hopes of forgetting how sad, violent, ugly, and useless their lives were.

Ugly and useless. I'd never thought of my life as having no meaning before we moved to the Lincoln Rooms, but during the three years we lived there, we learned more about sex and drugs and violence than anyone would ever need to know.

The hotel was like a little community, a microcosm of society, all by itself, and it didn't take us long to learn where we fit into the established pecking order: at the very bottom of the totem pole.

The grown men and their sons made fun of us, mostly because we had no father to protect us. Because I was the oldest boy, they would taunt me and tease me whenever I walked out the hotel door, challenging me to fight them. But when they started to use foul language regarding my two oldest sisters, I knew I had to do something to protect my family's honor.

It was all so difficult for me to understand then—our hates, our loves, the seasons, our youth; that everything in life is here for only a little while; that nothing lasts forever, except death. Death is forever, and the death of my father was the one thing I couldn't accept now, living at the Lincoln Rooms.

I would run from the men and beat my fists against a tree trunk, asking for strength and courage, knowing that my father would want me to protect our family. Then, back at the hotel, the men would shout at me and say, "Hey, little Mr. Vergara. Who beat you up?"

"Nobody beat me up," I said. "I fell against a tree, that's all."

"Oh, you fell against a tree?" Pedro Sanchez mockingly said as he slapped his thigh and stomped his foot into the ground.

"He fell against a tree, but the tree was bigger and stronger than he was, so it beat him up!" Sanchez loved to make fun of me, especially when there were others on the street with him. He laughed so hard at me that soon everyone else that was on the street was laughing along with him.

At that moment, this man looked to me just like the old Lincoln Rooms: dark and battle-scarred, ugly and unloved. As I looked at him, the image of the building standing behind him got all confused in my vision with the man himself. His eyelids seemed to me like the torn and fluttering curtains at the windows, his hair and skin like the threadbare carpets and the peeling wallpaper. He even smelled like the Lincoln Rooms, of sweat and urine and wine, as if it had spilled all over him.

The feeling I had, more than any other, was shame. I was ashamed of myself for not being able to fight back against this cruel bully, and I was ashamed for him too, because I remembered my father so well and knew how good a man could be. I knew to be a man also meant being kind and gentle and generous.

*You are not a man*, I thought. I trembled as I looked at Sanchez. *I'm not a man yet either, but I will be someday. Someday I'll be more of a man than you have ever been.*

I made that promise to myself without thinking about it. The idea that I would someday be a man gave me the courage to lift my head, straighten my back, and walk past my enemy into the hotel.

I ran up the stairs to our rooms, slamming the door behind me, and my mother gasped at the sight of blood on my fists and face.

"Where have you been, Mark?" she asked me. "Have you been in a fight?"

"No, not yet, but I will fight soon, very soon. Just you wait and see."

"But, Mark, why should you fight, son? Only bullies on the street fight. You are not a bully, Mark."

She was right. I was not a bully, but my mother was also oblivious to what was going on around her since the death of our father, or so it seemed to us children.

I wanted to fight, I honestly did, but every morning when I walked into the school yard and saw the same boys who lived on our block and in the hotel, I always bowed my head and walked past them without saying a word.

"Coward!" they called out to me. "Vergara is a coward!"

They would chant that over and over again so that I could still hear it ringing in my ears hours later. I felt as though I couldn't face it anymore without my father or an older man to help me, to love me and have faith in me. So I stopped going to school and spent my time down at the river, fishing or setting out traps to catch mink or muskrats.

I never thought they would come after me; I never realized that the teachers cared about one single student enough to notice he wasn't at school. I was sure they wouldn't miss one Vergara, since there were five of us who attended this school.

I had skipped two months, and one of the teachers, Mrs. Simpson, came to our rooms at the hotel and demanded to speak with me. My mother automatically called on me to explain what this lady was talking about. In a minute, I knew exactly why she had come.

"You have been truant, Mark, and you'll have to start coming to school again every day, or else."

*Or else what?* I thought, but I smiled and said, "Yes, Mrs. Simpson, I understand."

Since she knew my mother did not speak any English, Mrs. Simpson asked me to tell Mother what she had just told me.

For a moment I panicked, wishing I could come up with a good lie on the spot, but I was stuck, caught like a fish in a net, so I told my mother the truth. She never understood my reasons, though, as much as I tried to explain them to her.

"But, Mark, you have to go to school!" my mother said. "Tell the teacher you are sorry and promise to show up at school, every day. Go on and tell her!"

Mrs. Simpson was tapping her shoe on the worn carpet nervously and looking as if she wanted to leave the hotel as quickly as possible.

Then I surprised myself beyond my own comprehension. I suddenly turned to this tall, imposing woman, wearing a dark suit like a man's, and said, "I will go back to school, but not the Latino school. I will only go back if I am allowed to go to the Anglo school. In the Latino school, all they do is fight—that's the first and most important subject to learn. Well, I won't go there. I want to learn, not fight. Let me go to the Anglo school and I'll go every day, I promise!"

Mrs. Simpson mumbled something to herself and blurted out, "But you'll have to be tested for the Anglo school. You can only be accepted if you pass all the intelligence and aptitude tests. Will you take the tests, Mark?"

"Yes, of course I'll take them, and I'll pass them too—wait and see."

"All right," she said. "I'll notify the proper authorities. Be ready for them tomorrow morning."

"Thank you, Mrs. Simpson," I said, and I was grateful, although even then it seemed strange to me that I, who was just as American as she was, hadn't been allowed to go to the good school in the first place, when all the Anglos went there without having to get anyone's permission first.

I translated the results of our talk to my mother, and she was happy for me.

"Even if you don't pass the tests, Mark, I will still be proud of you for having stood up for yourself like a man! Your father would have been proud of you too, I'm sure!"

I passed the tests, and in just a few months I became an A student in the Anglo school. I really loved it, especially since I had fought for it myself, without having to use my fists to get it.

I wasn't half as lucky at home, since I had to go back there every day. I would bury my feelings in the back of my mind, I would pretend that I didn't see or hear what was going on, but I could never get rid of the problems I had there, and they built up until they reached a peak, forcing me to solve them.

That's how it was for our problem with Delores, my oldest sister. By this time, she was almost fourteen, and her body was filling out nicely, too nicely, since all the men at the Lincoln Rooms were after her, even the married ones. Even the oldest, ugliest ones would reach out and try to pinch her as she passed, but instead of hating the attention and being ashamed of it, Delores became proud of the new power she had found.

This power went to Delores's head. I don't know how much my mother was aware of during this time, since she preferred to be deaf, blind, and dumb to the bad things going on around her, and who could have blamed her? I only had to open my eyes in the morning and remember where I was to feel sick to my stomach and deeply sad in my heart.

My mother couldn't stop us from growing up, and I'm sure she didn't want to stand in our way. But I know that she regretted how quickly it had to happen.

One day when I came home from school, she asked me to come and sit down next to her. She said, "Mark, I have a very serious subject I want to discuss with you."

I could tell from the look in her sad brown eyes that something was wrong and that she would be asking me to help make it right again. She suddenly looked so old. It hit me like a slap on the face, or maybe I hadn't taken the time to realize how heavy a burden this new life had become for my mother; she was blind in one eye from the time she'd had smallpox as an infant, and she had to turn her head in an almost unnatural way when she looked at someone to get all of the person's face into her field of vision. But now it must have been a terrible strain on her good eye, because it was red and bloodshot; maybe she'd been crying.

"I want to ask you about your sister Delores," she said, "and I want you to answer me honestly. You understand, Mark?"

"Yes, Mamma," I said, trying to appear calm, even though I was beset by a mixture of emotions, all warring against one another suddenly in my heart. I wanted her to confide in me, since I was her oldest son, but I knew that I could never take my father's place for her, and I always felt small in comparison to his memory. My mother had built him up in her mind so that my father seemed like a god to her now.

"This evening, we are going to have a visit," my mother said, "from a man who will be asking permission for his son to marry Delores. When I saw him this morning, he was very polite, asking if he could come around this evening to discuss the matter. I wanted to say no right away, little one."

My mother had called me *little one*. She hadn't used that expression for many years.

"Yes, Mamma?" I asked, squirming in my seat and wanting to get up and leave her, since I felt it was her problem, not mine. But I wanted to be strong, so I stayed right where I was and waited for her to come to the point.

"I am against this marriage for a number of reasons, Mark. Delores is too young. The boy is young too, young and poor, and his father is an—his father rode with Pancho Villa, and that alone should be enough for me to say no to him, since he and your father were on opposite sides in the revolution.

"But he is a man, my son, and I am only a poor widow with six children. Oh, Mark, what am I going to do tonight when he comes here? Will you come and stand behind my chair and speak for me? Will you be the one to say no for me?"

My throat was suddenly so dry that I swallowed deeply, trying to force my fear back down into my stomach. I was afraid my voice would crack if I tried to speak, so I nodded to signify that I meant yes, and my mother threw her arms around me, weeping on my shoulder.

"Thank you, my son," she said. "I know your father must be smiling down at you now, since this is a wonderful thing you are doing for me, for Delores, for the family."

*Oh, dear God*, I thought. I could not say no to my mother, so I would now have to say it to a grown man. I could already see and hear his laughing at me, slapping his thighs like that bastard Sanchez, and laughing out loud at the twelve-year-old who was trying to act like a man.

After dinner that night, my mother and Delores quickly cleared the table and washed the dishes while I waited for Mr. Ortiz to come. I sat on the couch pretending to read a schoolbook. Inside, I kept thinking how ridiculous this request of my mother's was. I wondered if she knew how the men made fun of us and how absurd I would look, standing behind her chair.

I should have said all these things to her, but I didn't. I waited, thinking about all the boys who had ever called me a coward. Just then Mr. Ortiz was knocking at the door. "It's me," he said. "May I come in, Mrs. Vergara?"

She went to greet him and led him into the small front room. I stood up when he entered and bowed my head to him respectfully. Then my mother asked him to sit down, and she sat down too. I walked over behind her chair, as she had asked me to do, and tried to look as manly as I could, thinking of my father and trying to imagine him standing in my place.

He took his hat off and put it in his lap, turning it round and round as he spoke.

"So, as you must know, I have come to ask for your daughter's hand in marriage to my son, Luis," Mr. Ortiz said, getting directly down to business. He was polite enough, but even I was surprised that he hadn't engaged in some small talk first, by asking about the weather or the state of my mother's health. She and I were both silent as we stared at him. Then she turned to me, twisting her head around so that she could see my face, and said, "Mark, you may speak now."

I wanted to make the sign of the cross over my chest, in the vain hope that Jesus would come down from Heaven to help me at that moment, but I couldn't lift my hand up. I had been practicing a little speech as I waited for this moment, but it disappeared right out of my mind. I took a deep breath and said, "My mother has asked me to represent the family, sir, and it is our opinion that your son is an asshole, sir!"

It had just slipped out, and I was just as shocked as everyone else in the room was to hear it. Delores suddenly stepped out from behind the curtain that separated the kitchen from the living room and stared at me with her hands up over her mouth.

Mr. Ortiz smiled nervously. "I'm sure I didn't hear you correctly, young man," he said to me.

"Your son is an asshole!" I repeated, this time somewhat louder, gaining some confidence from the shock value of what I had already said. "He is unworthy of marrying my sister. You are all assholes."

Although I had imagined this man laughing at me, it had never occurred to me that he would get angry. His breath was coming quickly, and his face turned red, as little drops of perspiration formed at his forehead.

"You have insulted my honor, young man," he told me, "and if you weren't so young, I would have to challenge you to a fight." Then he stood up, put his hat back on, and walked over to the front door.

I really thought he was going to leave and that would be the end of it, but then Delores ran up to Mother.

"You can't let him do this, Mamma! You can't let him speak for me. No one ever asked me what I want, but I'll tell you now. I want to marry Luis. I don't ever want to pull another beet out of the ground, and if I stay here, I'll never get another chance to leave. Don't you see, Mamma? He wants to take me to California with him. He wants to take me away. It's the only way I'll ever get out of here!"

"Your daughter has a mind of her own, Mrs. Vergara," the man said, nodding with approval at Delores's independent spirit.

I even felt a little proud of her, since she had been courageous enough to say what was on her mind. I also felt a little sorry for her, realizing the truth in her words.

Then Mother stood up and said, "But you are too young, Delores, and you will have many chances to leave this horrible place. I know how horrible it is too. You may not know this, but I have spent many nights crying into my pillow since the death of your father, and since the death of your little sister. Do you think I am happy here, Delores? Do you think it's any better for me here than it is for you? What hope will I ever have of leaving this filthy place? You are young yet, and your whole life lies ahead of you."

"Yes, I'm young," she said, throwing her head back like a young colt. "And you are old, Mother. You may never have the chance to leave. This is my chance, and I want to take it!"

Then she ran into the children's room, crying into the dish towel that was still in her hands, and she slammed the door behind her. We stood there in shocked silence, hearing her sobs right through the door. When I turned to look at my mother, she had raised her hands up over her ears to block out the terrible sounds from the bedroom.

"I'd better be leaving now," Mr. Ortiz said, holding his hand out for my mother to shake it. But she just turned her head away and let him go.

Two weeks later, when she was getting the children ready for school in the morning, my mother found the note Delores had left for her on the kitchen table.

It is now midnight, and Luis will be meeting me on the corner in a few minutes, so by the time you get this, we will already be gone. I may not be a woman yet, but I will be, as soon as we get married. Then everything will be wonderful for me. We're heading for San Luis Obispo, California, and I will write to you as soon as we get settled. Please don't be too angry. Susanna will help you with the little ones from now on, and you will have one less mouth to feed! Good-bye from your Delores.

"One less mouth to feed?" my mother said, looking sadly at the children as she put their tortillas down in front of them. "But how will I feed the others, if you are not here to help me with the work of pulling the beets?"

She slumped down in a chair. I ran to her side and patted her gently on the shoulder. Even as I said, "We'll take care of each other," I was thinking that I, too, would one day be leaving my mother, as all of us would. One day, my mother would be all alone in the world.

# CHAPTER THREE

IT TOOK US five years to pay off all the family debts. It was five years that seemed like climbing up out of a hole in the ground, but I couldn't leave my mother until I knew she and the little ones had enough money to get them through the winter months. When the last cash voucher had been paid in full, I knew my time had come.

It was November of 1935 when I turned seventeen. The weather was so cold and bleak that I folded a thin blanket into a roll that I carried over my back, and I headed for the rail yard. With only fifty cents to my name and a few tacos in a paper bag, I walked through the snow and freezing rain. I knew only that I was going to California, a thousand miles away, to find a better life for myself.

A lot of people were on the move in those days: the Okies and Kansans who were abandoning their homes and farms to the great dust storm of the thirties and all the homeless and jobless men who became hobos, riding the rails in search of a job or a loaf of bread. When I joined them, I felt like a grain of sand on the beach, tossed about by the waves, lifted and then thrown down wherever the tide would take me.

There were so many of us I felt that our names and faces got all mixed up, and it didn't matter who we were anymore, who we had been, because we were now just hungry men, looking for work, carrying our most valuable possessions in our hip pockets.

Bill had a harmonica, and he could blow into it; Joe knew how to tap his feet in time to the music, and he could dance to it; and Jim could tell a good story, keeping the others around the campfires spellbound. But none of these valuables would bring them the price of a meal ticket, no matter how well they played or danced or told their wonderful stories.

That's why I felt we were all the same, brothers under the skin, because we were all just men, yearning for a job and a safe place to sleep. Luckily, I was strong, but even the young people didn't stay that way for long. If they did find work, they might end up earning only fifteen cents an hour, or a dollar and twenty cents at the end of a long, hard day of picking crops. And if they didn't believe in God, or if they didn't love life a lot, they might begin to wonder what they were doing on earth, living like dogs. That was why I wanted so desperately to get to California. It seemed like the end of the rainbow to me, and I hoped, like so many before me, to find my fortune there—if not in gold, then at least in a good job.


I learned a lot when I was riding the rails: how to make a sandwich last for hundreds of miles and how to stuff newspapers inside my clothes so that I wouldn't freeze at night. The blanket I'd brought along wasn't nearly enough to keep the howling winds away, let alone protect me from the ice that seemed to work its way under my skin like a knife. Stealing my way onto a freight train, sometimes while it was moving, wasn't an easy thing to do, but I learned—fast. I knew that I'd be lucky if I made it sixty miles without stopping or without being thrown off the train.

I got frostbite on one of my toes as we were passing through Soldier Summit in Utah. I didn't realize it until much later, since there wasn't any feeling at all in the toe—it just felt numb. I wished that the rest of my body had been numb; every time the train lurched forward or picked up speed, I could feel the vibrations come up through the boxcar and into my bones, even into my teeth. I had to try very hard to keep my mouth open, since I was afraid of biting my tongue.

Maybe I shouldn't have said that all the men riding the rails were like brothers. I mean it in the best sense of the word because being alone and out of work, with no money and no place to go, can make some men very bitter. I once jumped into a boxcar thinking I was alone, when suddenly I saw a man crouching in the corner like a wild animal. He growled at me and I was so afraid that I jumped off.

I would see men like that again, having lost the dignity of their manhood, but that was much later, in Southeast Asia. Poverty and misfortune do not always bring out the best in men; for some it seems to strip away their very humanity.

I'd never known real hunger before, but by the time I finally reached California, I was so hungry that I sold a sweater for fifty cents in order to buy a thirty-five-cent dinner at a Chinese restaurant. Then I had the strength to go on—to find my sister Delores, who was still living in San Luis Obispo. She had remarried and now had two children.

When I met a few men who were traveling south along the coast, I decided to travel with them. One of them heard that a person could always find a bit of leftover food in the refrigerator cars, so after searching through the boxcars, we finally found one with four crates of dried apricots spilled out onto the floor. We stuffed our pockets and ate our way down south, truly living off the fat of the land.

I felt that I was in heaven as soon as we got off the train. It had taken me three weeks to get to California, with many stops along the way, and I felt lucky indeed to have arrived without being shot at or chased out of town by the bullies with their billy clubs or thrown into jail for vagrancy, as so many of the other hobos were, especially the Black men, who didn't have a chance in those days.

I remember passing through a park in San Jose one night around midnight, and one of my fellow travelers pointed to a tree and told me that a Black man had been lynched there by a mob. I had seen many strange things for the first time in my young life: men sleeping with other men for the price of a dinner and grown men almost killing each other over a can of beans. But all these horrible images flew right out of my mind when I reached the town where my sister lived.

A stranger stopped me on the corner of Sycamore Drive. He asked me if I was looking for a girl.

"I'm looking for my sister," I replied, and he laughed, a twinkle in his eye.

"Sure, sure!" he said. "Well, you're going in the right direction!"

I walked slowly along the west side of Sycamore Drive, trying to find my sister's house, but all I could find was women! They were everywhere, one after another, all along the street.

I had never seen so many beautiful women! Redheads and blondes, brunettes and raven-haired beauties who called out to me as I passed them.

I soon discovered that the west side of Sycamore Drive was a red-light district in San Luis Obispo. Delores lived on the east side, and I was so close to the end of my journey that I started walking faster and faster, then trotted down the sidewalk like a horse, and finally I broke into a run, letting the whistles and laughter of the women fade out behind me. I didn't have the money to visit them, and maybe they thought I was afraid; maybe I was, but I kept telling myself I was almost there. I was almost home! I felt like a long-lost son when I reached my sister's doorstep.

I ran my fingers through my hair to make it look neater. My heart was beating quickly as I saw her through the window.

She pulled the curtain aside, threw her arms up in the air, and called out, "My brother! My brother is here!"

I have to admit that I was crying, but it didn't matter. I knew she wouldn't take it as a sign of weakness on my part.

Delores was crying as we hugged each other. For the longest time she sobbed on my shoulder as if she were still a child and I had suddenly reminded her of the past, of the old life she had left behind so many years ago, the old life I, too, had now fled.

She led me into her living room and introduced me to her new husband, Salome, and their two children. She started crying again and said, "I can't believe it is you, Mark; you're all grown up! Seeing you again is like being transported back to the past."

After she brought me something to eat and drink, she and her family crowded around my chair, asking me a hundred questions all at once.

Delores kept shaking her head in disbelief. "You look so much like Mamma," she kept saying. "I just don't believe it!"

It was true. I did look more like my mother than my father, but that was okay. Our mother had always been okay, even through the most difficult times in her life; it had never been easy for her, and I couldn't help thinking that she had never been lucky enough to live in the kind of house that Delores and her husband owned.

I was even more impressed when they showed me to a room of my own. It was small and furnished simply, but I had never slept in a room of my own before. I prayed to God that night that it wasn't all a dream that would go up in smoke the next morning.

I could hardly sleep that night, since the bed was so much softer than the freight train floors and the dirt roads I'd been sleeping on for almost a month.

The air that came in through the window felt as soft as silk, and I was grateful for every breath I took. I wanted to spend the rest of my life just lying there, breathing in the wonderful California air.

I had no trouble finding a few temporary jobs, first as a gardener, then as a woodcutter, a farmhand, and even a horse trainer. When I landed a regular daily job in a lumberyard, I was really happy and was able to purchase my first car, a Model A Ford roadster. It was the most beautiful car in the world! It even had a big Indian head on the radiator cap, and I would wax and polish that Indian head until it shined like a beacon.

My friends and I would load into the car and go dancing on Saturday nights in a little town named Arroyo Grande. On Sundays, we would all go to Pismo Beach, with a song on our lips and lust in our young bodies, hoping that the girls would be as willing as we were.

By the middle of 1937, I enlisted in the Civilian Conservation Corps, which was administered by the US Army and would give me the basis for my future career in the military. I didn't know then that I would ever fight in a world war, but somewhere in the back of my mind, I must have realized that the military would one day be my home.

I was sent to a camp in the Los Padres National Forest, east of the San Marcos Pass, and was assigned to the forest service, supervised by the forest rangers. My assignments varied from painter, welder, and cement worker to truck operator, construction-equipment operator, and many other jobs.

Some of the most important lessons I learned were how to live with other men and how to take a joke. Some men are funny when there are no women around; they do silly things like short-sheeting a man's bed so that he can't get his legs down into it or waking him up in the middle of the night, flipping on the lights, and shouting, "Everybody up! Short-arm inspection! Drop your socks and grab your cocks!"

I was truly naïve in those days, and everyone knew it, sending me out on fool's errands for left-handed monkey wrenches and something they called sky hooks. It didn't take me long to get wise, and in a way, I have to thank those guys for helping me grow up. Since my father had died when I was young, and also because I had no older brothers, I had never learned what it was like to follow orders. I did know that I could never become a leader of men until I had learned how to be a good soldier and do exactly what I was told to do.

My experience in the forest service turned out to be exactly what I needed to survive for the rest of my life, since it kept getting harder and harder all the time.

Before my enlistment was completed, I had obtained my high school diploma and had enrolled in the trade school in Los Angeles to study diesel engineering. I finished 50 percent of the course, and through school officials, I got a job as a truck driver based in Phoenix, Arizona.

As a truck driver, I hauled more than fruits and vegetables into Washington State, Colorado, and New Mexico.

One day in Phoenix, my boss called me in and introduced me to an Indian agent, who was in charge of procuring work for Indians living on the Navajo reservation. He had negotiated a deal with the Department of the Interior, Indian Affairs, for their employment.

I was told to go to Gallup, New Mexico, and turn north on Highway 666, on toward Shiprock, and to keep a sharp lookout for a man named Jack sitting in a black pickup truck. He would guide me to an Indian village, where I was to pick up approximately thirty Indians and haul them to Grants, New Mexico, to a carrot farm.

I finally met Jack and followed him into the desert for what seemed an eternity. To this day, I do not know how he knew where to go! There were no tracks and no road of any kind, just miles and miles of open desert covered with sagebrush and cacti. When we finally stopped, he blew his horn twice and took off. I never saw him again.

It was twenty minutes before I saw the first Indian coming down from the side of a canyon. He raised his right arm as a gesture of good-will and asked me if I was the one who would take his people to work. As I was answering him, he let out a yell that could be heard for miles around, and within minutes I had a truckload of Indians.

There was no discussion, but I knew I had more Indians than I was supposed to haul to Grants. There were so many women and children huddled in the rear of the trailer, I finally got a carton of cigarettes from my cab and bribed the men to move to the rear, asking the women to the front where it would not be so cold.

The wind began to blow really hard as I started to make tracks for the highway, and several times I had to stop, trying to search for my old tracks, which had already been covered by the desert sand. I turned to the most reliable source, the Indians, and soon they were guiding me back onto the highway.

I hauled these Indians many times after that, once to the Valley of the Sun, where the name complemented the weather. We became good friends, and I learned many things about their history and tribal customs. I would stop along the way to their destination of stoop labor and let them rest, and we would end up having a picnic as they sang and danced to the sun.

At the end of the journey, I always ended up leaving them in an old barn, but to me, it was better than the place I had picked them up from.

Many years later, while in the military, I visited my old trucking boss in Phoenix. He told me the Indians had saved their stoop labor money and had bought a herd of sheep, returning to the desert permanently.

"They asked about you often, Mark," he told me.

"I would visit them if I could remember the way," I said. But I never did.

Trucking was good for me, and every day, with every new thing I learned, I was moving closer to my future and my destiny, to that morning in December 1941.

# CHAPTER FOUR

I WAS SITTING in a movie theater in Phoenix when on the screen flashed: *Pearl Harbor has been attacked by the Japanese.* I had no idea where Pearl Harbor was, but I soon learned what was taking place all over the world.

I immediately joined the US Army Air Corps. I was sent to Fort Bliss, Texas, where I was processed and quarantined for three weeks. My basic training was administered at Sheppard Field, Wichita Falls, Texas.

In 1941, racial prejudice was rampant in the Army, especially at Sheppard Field. I was allowed to fight and maybe give my life for America, but because I was a Latino, as far as the Army was concerned, I was only allowed to perform general duty.

The Anglos who were running the processing section at Sheppard, were all activated National Guardsmen from Texas. They were a tight group, believing that some races were by nature superior to others. They denied me my rightful opportunity to take my training at the technical school, even though I scored very well on the tests. Other men were granted the right, some with lower qualifications than I had achieved. Most were good ole boys.

I requested to see my test scores, but the officer seemed inattentive, ordering me to my dormitory. I eventually did see them, when I was assigned to Geiger Field in Washington State, and I expressed my contempt in a self-satisfying way by volunteering to attend aerial gunnery school.

I learned ballistics, skeet shooting, range firing, machine-gun malfunctions, the use of flying equipment, the art of survival in the Arctic, and desert and sea survival. I was also trained in the basic knowledge of Morse code, how to fly and land a B-17, and how to deal with an emergency on board at high altitude.

I put my heart and soul into this training, and after I returned to my home base, I was immediately assigned to a crew as a tail gunner. When we were told that we had been picked to fly to the Pacific to join the Battle of Midway, we let out the loudest war whoops ever heard.

Going into combat always made me feel a jumble of emotions: excitement mixed with fear and the spirit of adventure. It also gave me a feeling of heightened reality. The knowledge that I might die any moment made me start to notice all the little details that go into a man's life. I grew quiet inside, listening to the sounds around me, watching everything very carefully, as if I didn't want to miss a thing, because life suddenly seemed very important to me. The idea that I might be instrumental in saving the lives of my fellow crew members gave a new meaning to my existence. I knew I was finally and absolutely a man.

When we were given leather jackets for summer flying and heavy wool-lined jackets and pants for the winter, we were already flying high, even though we hadn't taken off yet. At the last minute, all the ball turret and tail gunners were taken off the crew temporarily; we boarded a transport at San Francisco, heading for Hawaii. With Navy destroyers and cruisers along to escort us, we moved out into the bay to join the large convoy.

I'd never been on a ship in my life and began feeling sick even before we started moving at full speed. At least there was some compensation in store for me and my buddies. The nurses were up on the top deck, so were the officers. Guards were posted on the stairways to keep us troops from going up there, but they had never seen a flight jacket on an enlisted man. Mistaking us for officers, they let us pass, allowing us to visit the nurses for the longest time.

When we reached Pearl Harbor, parts of the harbor were still smoldering from the treacherous fires inflicted on the nineteen ships sunk or damaged. It was a devasting blow to me, a real slap in the face. I couldn't believe what I was viewing, staring down into the smoldering ruins that were once home to more than two thousand men. I wiped the drops of sweat off my forehead, then wiped my eyes, telling myself it was the tropical heat that was making me feel sick to my stomach.

I realized that I would have to learn to hate before I could actually kill a man. I thought I hated the Japanese, but there were lots of Chinese on the island. Some of them even wore signs around their necks saying, *I am Chinese, not Japanese.* But I couldn't really tell the difference, and when some Chinese were killed by mistake, it hit me that we, mankind, were involved in something unholy, something so powerful that it was impossible to put a stop to it. We'd been trained to think that we would be doing just the opposite and would be heroes for defending freedom throughout the world. But it was hard to tell the difference sometimes, especially when men were dying for what seemed like no reason at all.

My buddies and I were taken to Hickam Field and told to go to base supply, where we were issued pith helmets, side arms, and ammunition, along with large jungle knives. We all walked around looking like Jungle Jim!

We soon made contact with the rest of our crew, and for the next week or so made patrol flights, once stopping at an unnamed island to pick up a Marine general. The Japanese were giving our Marines hell, and I thought of my brother Carlos, who was somewhere in the Pacific. He was with the First Marine Division.

In March 1942, we were summoned to operations at Hickam and told to gather all our gear and fly back to the mainland, to Wendover Field in Wendover, Utah. This field was located on the edge of the Great Salt Lake Desert, a bleak, barren, and deserted area that was the new home of the 306th Bomb Group, 368th Squadron, of which I was now a member, part of the newly formed Heavy Bombardment Group that would soon become famous for their daring daylight bombing missions over enemy territory in Europe.

When our new B-17s were ready for action, we departed our base in Massachusetts, stopping in Gander Lake, Newfoundland, before we arrived at Prestwick, Scotland, at the Royal Air Force station there. The next and final leg of our trip took us to our destination, Thurleigh RAF station near Bedford, England. This was on the morning of September 2, 1942.

As we landed, the ground crew came out to meet us, realizing that the last time we'd seen them had been in Wendover, Utah. They told us they had traveled across the United States in railroad cattle cars all the way to Fort Dix, New Jersey, and had traveled overseas on the *Queen Mary*, landing in Liverpool after dodging U-boats all the way across the Atlantic.

As I lay in my bunk that first night in England, I had the strangest thoughts. If I died in combat, who would claim my body? If I was lucky enough to live through the war, who could I say I had done all the fighting for? It was all very disturbing to me. I lay awake for the longest time, and the war in Europe suddenly seemed to make sense to me. Of course, it occurred to me why: my father had been born in the valley of Arratia, in a Basque village in northern Spain; I realized I could be fighting to help save the lives of my own people, maybe even my own relatives.

My father's parents emigrated from the Basque Country to Mexico in the middle 1800s, settling in the small town of Santa Rosalía Camargo in the northern state of Chihuahua. My father was born in

1870 and raised on a ranch; he often spoke about his early days on the cattle ranch, stroking his long chin in reflection.

"At the time your grandparents came to Mexico, my son, the land was for the taking and every European who came to the New World stepped right in and got a piece of the action. The Vergaras were no different. They settled mainly in the northern states of Chihuahua and Durango, becoming quite influential in their buying and selling of cattle. One of your uncles was appointed to the governorship of the state of Durango by President Porfirio Díaz prior to the beginning of the revolution of 1910. When the revolution broke out, Díaz was exiled to Paris, France, and your uncle went with him because of the prerevolutionary feelings that existed in the United States at that time."

"Tell me more, please, Pappa," I would say to him, always looking directly at his wedge-shaped face and at his eyes, which would wander out to the horizon before he spoke again.

"As much as I hated the Villistas for their terrorism and the brutal ways in which they conducted themselves, I agreed with their aims and goals: to live in freedom, to live as free men. I simply didn't believe that you could steal a thing like freedom, and that's what they were doing, stealing it like robbers in the night."

"Is that why you and Mamma came to the United States, Pappa?" I knew the story, but I could listen to it a thousand times over.

"Yes, my son, for freedom from Pancho Villa and the noose around my neck." He would look directly into my eyes and place his hand upon my head, ruffling my hair with his fingers before speaking again.

"There were some who thought that coming from Spain made it easy for the Basques to assimilate themselves into the Mexican culture, but the Basques were not like any other Spaniards, just as our language has no Latin roots. We are an unusual people, my son, because of our shrouded origins and our untraceable language. We are a quiet and freedom-loving race, my son."

As I listened to my father speak, I realized the difficulty he must have had learning a new language he was not likely to use outside the home. It did not seem possible for the Basque language to be totally unrelated to any other language in existence; it had to be traced back to a starting point somewhere, so where was it? I asked my father.

He smiled before answering me, stroked his long chin again, and said, "We are the oldest surviving social group in Europe, my son, perhaps descendants of a late Paleolithic people. We have baffled linguists over our ancient language, sometimes compared to Hungarian, but they will never trace it, my son, for it is untraceable, the most difficult of all languages on earth."

"I will go to the Basque Country someday, Pappa," I answered him, knowing that deep in his heart it was what he had always wanted to do since coming to the United States.

"Yes, yes, my son, you must go there while you are still young, and visit your family in the valley of Arratia; the last I heard, some had gone to Pamplona, but they will know you, Mark; identity is unmistakable. A Basque is a Basque."

My father wasn't an educated man in the strict sense of the word, but he was well informed about the world and its people. His philosophy was this: "Always talk to someone smarter than yourself, otherwise you will never learn anything. If you talk, and talk to someone who is dumb, then you'll end up as dumb as he is."

"How did you meet Mamma, Pappa?" I asked. "And how did you escape the noose of Pancho Villa?"

"Listen carefully, and I will tell you the story, my son," he said. "Your mother was a beautiful but frail woman when I first met her. It seemed a miracle to me that she had survived at all, since she had been struck down with smallpox as a very young child. There was always something otherworldly about her, as if her recovery from the deadly disease had been an act of grace, bestowing a special aura about her. She is mestiza; her parents were half Comanche Indian, one-third

Kiowa, and the rest Spanish. I was a cattle buyer for a wealthy German rancher. His name was Julio Mullar, and it was said of him that he owned most of the land between Juárez and Chihuahua City. Your mother was the nanny, or governess, for Mr. Mullar's children, living in Mullar's large hacienda. Of course, I was the best man for the job, the best man in all of Mexico."

My father and I laughed together as he bragged a little about his position, but I knew he must have been the best man for Mr. Mullar.

"It was the most exciting and most dangerous time in my life. Your mother and I had been married in the large church in Chihuahua, and Mr. Mullar had given us a marriage fiesta at his hacienda; it was all so exciting and joyous. It was in April of 1914 when I met Pancho Villa and was almost hanged."

"Why, Pappa?" I asked.

"Villa and his men had already taken control of most of the northern cities, including most of the towns in Durango and Chihuahua; I was on one of my cattle-buying trips for Mr. Mullar. I had already bought and paid for the cattle and had arranged for the train to meet them at a siding. I had no way of knowing that Villa's men would be riding on top of the railroad cars and shooting at the cattle for their pleasure and sport. When I arrived at the scene, all my cattle were dead. I demanded to speak to Villa himself; I could have been killed! It's only by the grace of God, as you must believe, my son, that my life was spared. I got into such a fight with Villa. I was then taken to jail and sentenced to be hanged the next morning."

My father paused as if to thank God again for saving his life, and I nudged him and asked him to continue telling me about this dangerous episode in his life.

"I was a smart man, my son; as always, I had taken my young assistant, Jose, with me on this trip. Jose got word to Mr. Mullar that I was in trouble, terrible trouble. Luckily for us all, Mr. Mullar agreed to pay for my release, even though he had lost his cattle and the money he had spent to buy them."

"Did Villa let you go right there and then, Pappa?"

"We were warned to leave Mexico within twenty-four hours, and I was happy to do so, if only for a little while, until it was safe to return. After buying my freedom, Mr. Mullar and his family brought us across the border, and we made a temporary home for ourselves in Las Cruces, New Mexico."

I was listening intently, not knowing what it must have been like for my father to be saved from the brink of death. He was actually standing on the gallows when his life was miraculously spared. I sat looking at the man I loved and respected and wondered what made him go up to Pancho Villa and start a fight in the first place, since in a way, he was putting the noose around his neck by walking into the lion's den and demanding justice. I think he did it because he was a Basque.

"Why did you never go back to Mexico, Pappa?"

"Mr. Mullar asked us to go back with him about a year later, my son, but I could still feel the noose around my neck, if you know what I mean, and I just didn't want to meet the hangman again. Besides, we had said good-bye to the past, son. We were taking the chance of not doing so well here, but everything we did in the old country was for the Mullars; we were fed and clothed with his money, and the house we lived in belonged to him. Even the peppers and tomatoes in your mother's garden belonged to our patron. By the time your oldest sister, Delores, was born, the United States had already joined the war in Europe, and it was clear to me that there was such a thing as a good war and a bad war. To my mind, America was fighting a good war, but Pancho Villa and his kind were not. As a man you have to make these choices, and then you must stick with your decision and see it through to the end."

I remember shouting: "Good war—bad war. Stick with your decision and see it through to the end."

My buddy Liscav was shaking me. "Hey, Mark, you okay, buddy?"

I awoke with a start, looking up at him. "I must have been thinking out loud," I said. "Where the hell are we?"

"We're in England," he answered me. "Don't you remember landing here? Boy oh boy, that must have been some dream, Mark!"

I lay back down in my bunk. The room was constantly lit by the flare from matches being struck. Many cigarettes glowed in the dark. Not much sleeping went on. I was not alone with the thought that the rolling East Anglian countryside would soon become a vast staging area for the greatest air armada ever to be assembled on the face of the earth.

# CHAPTER FIVE

🐂 IT WASN'T LONG before we were an active group. Although the US Army Air Corps was going ahead with its plans to run bombing missions in full daylight, the RAF personnel lacked the proper armament to defend themselves during the day, so they were operating mostly at night, although they supported our planes by acting as escorts in their Spitfires. Unfortunately, they could bring us only as far as the French coast and would then have to return for refueling. We met our moment of truth during our bombing missions deep in French territory, since the Germans would attack us all the way in and then all the way out again.

The beauty of the B-17 was in its performance, and it was designed for a single purpose: the precision bombing of strategic targets in the full light of day. It was the prime weapon of the Eighth Air Force during the entire war because it was able to penetrate deep into enemy territory, with the capacity to level the German armament factories without suffering critical losses. At least, that's how it was seen in theory. In practice, we were fighting a war of attrition. Whoever ran out of planes and men first would be the losers.

Many B-17s never came back; many came back with great damage, with dead crew members, and with others in the process of dying. By the end of the war, some forty-five hundred bombers and more than forty-three thousand men would be lost in the awesome struggles in the skies over occupied Europe and Germany. The bloody saga of the Eighth and Ninth Air Force was enacted in a little more than three years, from the first experimental probe in August 1942 until the final ceremonial missions in 1945.

The German fliers were very brave too, often flying against even higher odds than the Allied pilots who flew against the Luftwaffe in the Battle of Britain. This unrelenting savagery staged in the bizarre and unnatural arena of high altitudes and subzero temperatures meant that the young fliers were often glamorized above and beyond their ability to live up to the price they were asked to pay.

This letter was written to me by a survivor who was a friend of mine. It was dated January 10, 1946.

Trying to forget, I guess, is what caused me to neglect answering your letter. I don't believe it's actually a weakness in me. I still have bad dreams, still can't sit through a war movie and I still go to pieces when I retell the story of 2nd December 1942. But here it is. The first shell that hit the ship came from straight in the rear. It was a 20mm and it hit me. Not seriously, it didn't explode, and I didn't lose consciousness. From then till I got out, I heard the steady sound of machine guns and 20mm cannon fire. What I heard of the 20s was their explosion. I smelled no gunpowder, so none of our guns got a chance to fire. When I finally got out, the ship was a furnace—on fire from just rear of the nosewheel to the tail and with both wings ablaze too. I bailed out with my chute not hooked on but held in my arms. It was a chest-type chute. We were at about twenty-two thousand feet. After one unsuccessful attempt at pulling the ripcord, I had to open the thing with my fingers before the chute finally opened. I had fallen around 17,000 feet and the ground seemed very close. It was only a mile off. After the chute opened, I watched the ship. It broke in half and tumbled. I saw the front half hit the ground and blow up. If I had been in that ship a minute longer, I don't know how I could have lived through that hell and still be alive. But I did. I lived through it.

Falling seventeen thousand feet, clutching an unopened parachute. That was the part that really got to me. Even though I didn't experience it myself, I had visions of my friend falling through the sky, and somehow they got all confused with little Rosalie, falling down the well. I soon learned the kind of fear my friend had described. Fear I'd never dreamed of before.

As a tail gunner I had to squeeze myself into a tiny space with my legs up practically under my chin and only a thin layer of plastic between me and the sky, let alone being chased by the Luftwaffe and watching them come straight at me.

We had no radar sights at that time, so all combat missions were flown by celestial navigation, and the weather over the primary target had to be clear for the bombardier to use his bombsight effectively. We each had to fly twenty-five missions before we could be sent back home, and every time we went out, the Luftwaffe seemed to be getting better at knocking our planes out of the air. There was a crack German fighter squadron stationed at Abbeville, France, which we nicknamed the Abbeville Kids, that would attack us head-on in formation. You could usually figure when they had gone through us, because you could see two or three Fortresses staggering, rolling, and then falling out of formation. If we had the time, we would count the number of crew members bailing out.

I don't think that I'm much braver than the next man, but I never knew what real bravery consisted of until I had flown on the low-altitude raids, going after the U-boats in their pens. Protected by eight-foot-thick walls, these pens were practically impenetrable, and the Air Force had come up with a plan to discontinue the use of traditional high-altitude bombing and to try to skip bombs at the U-boats instead. They dropped them in the water, hoping that they'd skip over the water and then explode once they entered the pens. The only problem with the plan was that it failed as miserably as the conventional bombing attempts had.

Theoretically, by flying as low as possible, we would avoid flak from both the high and low positions, but in practice, we got it from both the top and the bottom. We were never free of it. We flew so low that we could see the French farmers waving at us from the ground. The rationale was that we would avoid German radar by staying below twelve thousand feet, but according to our pilot, we got as low as five hundred feet over the English Channel. I sometimes had the feeling that if I stuck my hand out of the plane, the way I might if I were sitting in a boat, it would dip into the water. If we were flying so low that we could see the U-boats, then it should have been obvious to the higher-ups that the Germans could see us.

I made it through even the most horrible attacks, the worst of which was over Saint-Nazaire. I remember turning my head suddenly and seeing a bomber get a direct hit on the nose. It rolled over with a crewman hanging by one leg, and then the whole crew went down. Then I heard our pilot come in over the intercom to the bombardier.

"Get rid of the bombs, and let's get out of here!"

When we headed out to sea, everybody started yelling at me, all at once. "Mark, Mark! They are coming at twelve o'clock high!" Then someone else shouted, "No, no, they're at three o'clock level!" They were all over the place, and someone else shouted, "Look out, tail gunner, they're above you!" I started saying "Hail Mary, full of grace," over and over again, and fired my twin fifties in every direction until we had finally made it safely away.

The pilot made a right turn and headed back to England. There were planes scattered all over the sky as far as the eye could see, and that was the end of the famous bombing-at-low-altitude theory.

Most of the guys I'd known in Wendover, Utah, never made it back home. I still have pictures that were taken of the group, and every time I look at them, it's almost as if I can hear their voices calling out to me again, in laughter and in pain, as if their spirits lived on in the world long after they were gone. It just wouldn't make any sense to me at all if that weren't true.

Sometimes it was even harder coming back from a mission than going out with our hopes up as high as the planes would take us, because sometimes when we came back and would stand in the doorway to our crew barracks, we would see the lines of empty beds, knowing that they'd never be filled again by the same men who had gone up with us in the morning. It always reminded me of a grave-yard, those beds with their bare mattresses rolled up, showing the springs of the cots underneath. It was terrible to go to sleep at night with those empty beds on either side of me and no buddy to talk to or swap cigarettes with.

We couldn't help making friends, even if we told ourselves not to get too attached to anyone. One guy was simply liked better than another, and I wanted to spend as much time with him as possible, since any day might be my last day too. I couldn't cry when they were shot down into the water or burned up in an exploding plane. I couldn't even say good-bye when I went out to the plane in the mornings, because I never knew, from one day to the next, whether this day would be my last day on earth.

I thought of my father often during those flights over Germany and crisscrossing the English Channel, like homing pigeons sent out to deliver a message full of bombs, and then heading right back for home. I thought of him with a noose around his neck, about to be hanged by Pancho Villa's men. He wouldn't have cried either.

I thought that my father had been even more brave during the last years of his life, a tall, proud man keeping his pride and dignity even as he kneeled on the ground, pulling beets for a few dollars a day. Sometimes, when I thought I would die up there in the sky, I thought of my father's bravery as he struggled against the cancer eating him alive, and I drew courage from his memory.

I did a lot of thinking alone in my tail-gunner position, especially when we first headed out in the early morning hours in beautiful formation, like great-winged birds flying south for the winter. *If I get it in the sky*, I thought, *I'll go straight to Heaven. They'll shoot me dead, and I'll never even feel myself landing. I'll fly straight upward, and my feet will never hit the ground.*

I'd talk to Pappa too, sometimes, in my most private thoughts. *Well, Pop*, I'd think, *if I've gotta die, then I might as well do it in a blaze of glory, right? You'll be proud of me; yes, you will.* I was so young then. I believed in those words like *glory* and *bravery* and *heaven*. A lot of the other guys believed in them too, and I don't think we would have been able to fight in the war if we didn't have those ideals to live by.

They weren't just words; they stood for all the people who Hitler wanted to kill and enslave. They weren't just words when we remembered why we had been sent or had volunteered to fight in the first place. And they weren't just words when the tide was beginning to turn and our side was beginning to win. That came later. Now we were taking a terrible beating and were losing a considerable number of aircraft, especially running bombing missions over places like Regensburg, Schweinfurt, and Wilhelmshaven. But we had to keep going out, day after day, to try to put an end to the German war machine.

We got a good taste of it when our target was the shipbuilding yards and U-boat pens at Bremen. That day our plane was Tail-End Charlie on the way there, but we were in the lead on the trailing element. That day I was flying in the upper turret position as engineer, and before we realized what was going on, the planes on either side of us were hit and lost. Then our number two and three engines had to be feathered because of direct hits by flak, and the plane was shaking so much that I spun the turret around once and felt myself floating.

My feet came off the floor and I tried with all my strength to get myself loose, but the centrifugal force kept me pinned inside the turret. When I was finally able to climb out and go to the forward part of the cabin, I saw the pilot and the copilot with their feet up on the dashboard, pulling back on the sticks with all their might. We were falling so fast that my legs began to buckle under me, and I thought I was going through the floor.

Then everything happened very quickly. We leveled out at ten thousand feet, but in a minute, we were diving down to sea level, and I was pinned in the turret again, right in the center of Bremen Harbor.

As we headed out, the pilot informed us that he couldn't maintain altitude, and we had to jettison everything we could lay our hands on—flying suits, machine guns and receivers, ammo belts, and anything that wasn't nailed down to the hull. Then we began climbing again, but our number one engine began sputtering, and the pilot said we'd be landing in the water, if he could manage.

"Strap yourselves in good and tight," he said.

It was a miracle that we made it, and we were all so excited when we settled down that we jumped into the water with our Mae Wests inflated. The pilot and the copilot got out through their windows and stood up on top of the plane like big-game hunters with their feet up on an elephant. Since the water was so shallow, the plane didn't sink and they only got wet up to their ankles. In a few minutes, the Royal Air Force air/sea rescue teams arrived to pick us up, and then we returned to base. They already had us listed as missing in action.

On one particular evening, as we made our way back to the squadron area after an evening in Bedford with the locals in the pub, we noticed a lot of activity on the flight line and knew that a mission was coming up.

One of my buddies was a young guy from New York by the name of Jeremy Bernstein. We made quite a pair, the Latino and the New Yorker, but we'd been together almost from the beginning, and it was just as surprising to me as it was to Jeremy that we were both still alive.

That night, as we lay awake in our room, watching the tiny flares from the lights of cigarettes all around us, Jeremy asked me if I was asleep.

"No," I replied, laughing, wondering if he actually expected to get an answer from me if I'd been sleeping.

"So where do you think our next raid is going to be?" he asked, rolling over on his side to get a better look at me from the arc lights coming through the window.

"Who knows?" I answered.

"If we keep going any deeper into Germany, we'll end up in Poland."

"That would be all right with me," I told him. "Maybe we could just keep going east until we make it all the way around the world and end up in the States again."

"Yeah, we could land on top of the Empire State Building," he enthusiastically replied. "I'd love to show you around, Mark. We'll do all the regular kinds of touristy things, okay? I'll take you to the Statue of Liberty and Radio City Music Hall, and then we can go uptown to hear some jazz, if you like that kind of music. Do you?"

I could just make out his shadow in the dim light. He was two years younger than I, twenty-three, but I felt as if I'd seen a lot more of the world than he had. Sure, he was from the big city. He'd been born in Brooklyn and practically grew up, as he kept telling me, in Ebbets Field. Sure, he came from the biggest, most important city in the world, but he'd never hopped a freight train or eaten cold beans out of a can. He'd never witnessed a murder, and I had, although I could hardly say I'd witnessed it, since I was hiding under a bed at the time.

"All I really saw were two pairs of feet," I said as I explained the story to him. "They were scuffling around together. If it hadn't been for the punching and groaning that came afterward, you might have thought these two pairs of feet were dancing together. Anyway, I must have been very young, since I don't remember anything leading up to the fight. I'm not even sure where I was, except that I'd gone somewhere with my father, and he'd put me into someone's bed. When I heard all the commotion outside the door, I quickly slipped under the bed and waited for the fight to stop. But it didn't." Jeremy loved my stories, so I continued.

"I stayed under the bed the whole time, even after one of the men slumped onto the floor. I remember seeing the other pair of feet stand back, then go and kick the dead man, and then hurry out of the door."

"Aw, you're just making that up," Jeremy said. "It sounds as phony as a three-dollar bill to me."

"No, I'm not!" I told him, sitting up and feeling a shiver suddenly run down my back. "I'm even afraid to look under my bed now; there might be a dead man under it." I had to convince him I was telling the truth.

"Okay, then what did you and the dead man do?" He rolled over onto his back again and stared up at the ceiling. "Did you ask him for the next dance?"

"I didn't do anything!" I said. "I just stared at the guy. There was a terrible wound on the side of his head, and a little river of blood was pouring out of it. I couldn't move an inch; I could hardly breathe, and I just kept watching the blood pour out of him. Then some other men came running into the room. They picked the dead guy up and dragged him up onto the bed—the one that I was under—and they put him on top of the bed, right above me; that's when I jumped out of there. When I saw my father's face, I was so glad that I just ran over to him and hugged him real tight."

"Humph!" was all Jeremy said.

"Listen, you don't have to believe me," I said. "But why would I make up a story like that? Just to impress you about how dangerous my childhood was? It wasn't all that dangerous, since mostly, all I remember is kneeling down on the ground, picking those damned beets with the sun beating down on me. Ha! Get the joke? With the sun beating down on me?"

I started laughing foolishly, nervously, with the sudden thoughts and the realization that Jeremy and I would be going up again in a few hours.

We were both quiet for a while, and then I heard him say, "I believe you Mark, and I'm sorry you had to see it, as a kid, I mean. I'll bet it was rough."

"Nah, it wasn't too bad," I told him, lying down again. "I haven't thought about it in years, although I used to wake up a lot in the middle of the night, just after my father died. And I'd get them turned around in my dream. I'd hear the men coming, duck down under the bed, and see their feet and the bottoms of their pants moving around in front of me. At one point, they were standing so close to the bed that I thought they'd fall down on it. Then when it was all over, it turned out that my father was the dead man, in my dream, anyway. That's when I would wake up, since I didn't have anyone to run and hug."

"Well—we know what that means," Jeremy laughingly said. "Something to do with Oedipus wanting to kill his old man and marry his mother!"

"Hey, that's a mean thing to say."

"Mean?" he said, taking the gum out of his mouth and rolling a piece of paper around it. Jeremy was very neat, and we joked about it a lot. He put the piece of paper in his shoe, so that he could throw it away in the morning. Then he said, "Are you going to tell me that you never once wanted to kill your father?"

"You're just crazy!" I loudly replied, and some of the guys down the line told me to quiet down. So I leaned down closer to Jeremy's bed and whispered just loud enough for him to hear me. "You're just crazy. I loved my father. Anyway, maybe he died before I was old enough to want to hurt him. Jesus, Jeremy, how could you ever think such a thing?"

"You're funny, Vergara," he said to me. "Why don't you just go to sleep now, okay? We'll only be getting a few hours until it's time for you-know-what."

"But I can't go to sleep after a guy tells me that I wanted to kill my old man. What does it mean, Jeremy?"

"Listen, if I explain it to you, will you let me get some sleep?"

"Sure," I said.

"Then just listen to me, you dodo bird! Every kid hates his father at some time in his life. It's only natural, and it's nothing to be ashamed of. It's all part of growing up, and it doesn't mean that you'll end up as a murderer or anything like that. It's just, well, it doesn't even mean anything, except he wants to get his father out of the way, so he can have his mother all to himself."

"His mother?" I shouted out.

"Will you shut up, Vergara?" the guy on the other side of me yelled. "For Christ's sake! We're going to get killed tomorrow, so will you let me sleep a little bit first? Jesus!"

"If you're going to be killed tomorrow," I said, turning to face Little Joe, as we called him, "then what difference does it make if we sleep tonight or not?"

Then I turned back to Jeremy, but he was waving his hand at me to let me know he wanted me to leave him alone now. I nodded a few times as if I understood.

I closed my eyes and tried to sleep, and I guess I had to admit to myself that Jeremy was right, in a way. I hadn't thought about it in a long time, because I'd always had the idea that I hated my father for dying, not for living! But there was a time when he killed my little calf, Joey, and I knew I wanted to kill him then.

I was only four years old when Mr. Froman gave me the little steer. My calf was exceptional at birth and would follow me everywhere. I fed him, groomed him, and cleaned him every day. As he grew, he became very large and very strong and would allow me to ride him. Then the day came to butcher him. I really made a scene. Father was preparing everything needed for the task, and I went to him crying, asking why he had to kill my beautiful steer. He said it was needed food for the winter. I told him I wasn't hungry and promised I would never eat again. I pleaded for Joey, but Father went ahead and butchered him. I did not eat any of the meat and would not speak to my father for a very long time.

I fell asleep. Three and a half hours later we were on our way to Emden, Germany, and I remembered my dream. I was a little boy, and my father was in his coffin. I was standing at his feet, with my head bowed, and I said to him. "It's all right, Pappa. I'll take care of things. Everything will be all right now, and you'll be proud of me. I'm sorry about the way I acted over Joey. I know now you had to do it, Pappa. I'll miss you so much. I am strong and will draw on your strength."

# CHAPTER SIX

SITTING AND WAITING to reach ten thousand feet before putting our oxygen masks on, and while the Forts assembled in formation, was always the boring part of a mission. We were again Tail-End Charlie, or as some called it, Purple Heart Corner. We were the far ship on the outside, and lowest in the formation.

One of the guys in the crew—we called him the Wiz—was a real joker, and he reminded us what the Spitfires looked like. "For God's sake, don't shoot any of them down," he said over the intercom. "They'll never forget it, and when they have to escort us again, they'll tell us all to go to hell."

I was cleaning my guns and checking the ammo belts when I suddenly realized how very clear it was becoming outside. As far as I could see I had an unobstructed view. I looked again and got a real bad feeling. None of the missions were ever easy, but this particular day was too clear, unusual for February in Europe. I rechecked my twin fifties again and got ready for the onslaught that was sure to come before the bomb bay doors were opened and the two words that we all waited for—"Bombs away"—came, followed by relief and "Get the hell out of here!"

"Everyone on your toes," the radio sounded. "We have visitors. Position check, let me hear you guys."

Our pilot always did this, wanting to hear the ten voices from within the ship. We all checked in, and I started to sweat as Peterson, our pilot, sounded off over the radio again.

"Flak coming in up ahead, up at the lead group. They're throwing it at us now. Fighters coming one o'clock high—pick 'em up, gunners."

The ship was vibrating from the turret, nose, and my tail guns firing back at the fighters' attack. Surrounding us were large black puffs of clouds from the flak, each spewing death and destruction to the B-17s should they connect. Each time I'd fire, my heart pumped that much faster, and as the sweat ran off of my face and we got closer to our target, I prayed for me and my crew, for this was the worst part of the mission.

"Bomb bay doors open—make sure there's nobody under us—check to make sure they're open—nobody slid under us?"

The bombardier was now flying the plane. I waited for the message and the relief of the words—"Get the hell out of here!"

The fighters came again as the bomb bay doors came up and were locked. Our pilot asked if we were all okay.

We all answered in a clear ungarbled voice.

There were quite a few planes in trouble now. Two had their engines on fire, and as we watched them and heard the voices on the radio, we realized they were from the lead group and were trying desperately to stay with their own guys.

"Slide under us," Peterson said to them, "so we can cover you."

They got between us and their own group when the eager fighters spotted them. The FW-190s dove in from the rear of the ailing planes and attacked in force with their guns, finally forming a large circle around them and hitting them from every angle imaginable.

We were now approaching the sea, and the two B-17s didn't stand a chance. As we watched the ships go down, the crew were still firing their guns, and the last thing I saw were the blasts from the top turret gunner as I watched the ships go under the water.

We were all suddenly very silent. We usually were on the way back to Thurleigh, watching the coastline and thanking God we had made one more.

I sometimes thought I should have joined the infantry because the fighting I did, caged up in a flying target, was like painting a bull's-eye on my chest and walking into a shooting range.

I came pretty close to dying on another mission, even before we left the hardstand. This nonflying, know-it-all intelligence officer showed up in the briefing room and pointed to a map with a red ribbon on it. He calmly explained to us that this was the ball-bearing plant in a town called Schweinfurt that we had never heard of before and then told us to expect heavy fighter opposition with intense flak. Some of us looked at one another, knowing one another's thoughts. Why couldn't the bastard have been honest and told us, You're going to get your asses shot off today, men!

*This is it*, I thought. *They will mow us down like blades of grass.*

The intelligence officer who briefed us before we went out on a mission would try to work us up into a feeling of righteous indignation that the Germans were fighting like the devil on both fronts and they were going to take over the world if we didn't do something about it. When he said *we*, we knew who he meant! He meant us and not him, since he got to stay behind and brief the next group of fliers, if we didn't make it back alive for tomorrow's mission.

We got worked up all right, but what were we supposed to do with it, belted into our seats like babies in high chairs? After those of us who were Catholics received the sacraments from the priest, we made our way to the hardstands, where the Forts were parked. The ground crews swarmed all over the B-17s, working while it was still pitch-dark, refueling, doing last-minute maintenance, and loading the bombs into the bomb bays. We picked up our machine guns and put them in the receivers, attaching their ammunition belts and checking to see that everything else was in order.

Then we were driven back to the Quonset huts, where cots had been provided for us to lie down until it was time to take off. There were always flight delays in England because of the uncertainty of the weather. They put us on hold over and over again. If I ever felt like biting my fingernails, this was the time for it. It was an inner fear, like stage fright; when actors pace around behind the curtain or in their dressing rooms before a performance, the tension seems to build up until it can't do anything but explode. That's how it was with me, anyway. I didn't know about the others, and it was hard to tell, since we were all so quiet. We were quietly waiting to put our heads in the noose.

That was part of it too, the feeling that we were doing it to ourselves, like volunteering to put an arm into a bagful of snakes. But whether we'd volunteered or been drafted, it didn't make any difference in the end, since there were no alternatives for us now. We no longer had the right or the opportunity to make a choice.

I knew it was wrong of me to let my fear build up, but I'm sure all the crew had similar feelings, even though it was never openly discussed. In those quiet moments before the flares went up and it was time to go, I went to war with myself. I imagined the most horrible death for myself, such as I had seen many times as other crews had gone down while I watched. It was horrifying.

Long before sunlight broke onto the field, and while we waited for the trucks to take us to the planes, I always said a little prayer for myself and my good friends:

Captain Peterson, our pilot, was a really nice fellow from Toledo, Ohio; his copilot, Captain Wiznewsky, who hailed from Chicago. We called him the Wiz since he always managed to bring a hard salami on board with him for every mission.

Jeremy, our ball turret gunner; Pete Raynor, the bombardier, who was so crazy about Betty Grable that we ended up nicknaming him Betty's Bomber; our young navigator, Sal Rizzo, from Detroit—we called him Slim Sal.

Little Joe Blackman and Big Moe Massey, the two waist gunners; Ed Caputo, whom we nicknamed Head Set Ed, our radio operator;

and Hard Harry, our engineer, who was a slow-talking Southerner with a heart as hard as his job called for. Ten of us in all.

I'd get these pictures in my mind of getting shot down over some two-bit farming village, with no strategic munitions plant or steel-manufacturing complex or anything important in it at all, just cows and manure and stacks of wheat. That's where we'd get it, and then I'd see us falling out of the sky like hailstones in a storm, except that we were on fire, blazing a trail of smoke and hellfire on our way down, flaming so bright and hot that we'd light up the sky like a torch, coming to earth in a potato field or smack in the middle of a herd of cows.

Sometimes I'd imagine that I could see the men as they'd been when they were boys, ten-year-olds with freckled faces and missing front teeth, with slingshots and marbles in their back pockets. I would wonder how it was for them to go to school, to have caught a frog or a snake in a shoebox and brought it home to frighten their sisters or their mothers. Did they dream of being soldiers when they grew up?

None of us were heroes, or maybe I should say that the only heroic thing we did was to go out on a mission knowing that the odds were one in three that we'd ever come back alive.

It was time to go. We were finally off, headed for Schweinfurt with a total of 291 bombers. Halfway across the English Channel, Captain Peterson came on the intercom, instructing the gunners to try out their guns by firing short bursts. Pete Raynor went back to the bomb bay and pulled the pins, arming all six of them, making sure that he secured the pins so that the interrogating officer would see that the bombs were leaving the plane armed and ready. In the event that we should abort the mission, it would become necessary to salvo the bombs over friendly territory; then we would have to replace the pins in the fuses so the bombs wouldn't go off when they were dropped,

The weather was great over the Channel, which was good for navigating but also let the Germans see our vapor trails for hundreds of miles. The Eighth Air Force wanted us to keep in close formation, flying in what they called a *combat box*, but turbulence buffeted the planes, and there was always danger of collision, flying so close together. The altitude caused us physical anguish that was almost as bad as the fear. At twenty-six thousand feet, the temperature was around sixty to seventy degrees below zero, and we had to keep reaching up and squeezing the tube on our oxygen masks, since the moisture in our breath would condense and freeze, which would cut off the flow of oxygen. We certainly didn't want to die from the very equipment that was supposed to keep us alive.

The B-17s were bombers, not fighters, and as soon as our fighter escorts had to turn around and leave us, the Germans started hitting us with their Messerschmitts and Focke-Wulfs. We were five miles high with no place to hide and had lost thirty planes while we still had two hours to go to reach our target. By the time we got there, we found the sky filled with the jagged metal from the flak guns.

The run over the target was called the *bomb run*, and since we had to fly straight and level for about fifty miles, we were sitting ducks. The German ack-ack gunners were so good they could get our altitude, speed, and direction and put a shell in us within forty seconds, so we held our breath until we heard Pete shout out, "Bombs away!"

Then we would start the evasive action, trying to outmaneuver the flak gunners from down below. It was always amazing to me how we managed it, dodging first to the left and then seeing a cloud of black puffs appear where we had been just a few seconds before. Then we'd move to the right and the same thing would happen, so that we ended up dancing our way out of there like a bull in a beehive.

The bomber itself wasn't even that much protection against enemy fire, since the armor plate had been taken off to allow for maximum bomb weight. Even the infantry can dig itself into a foxhole to avoid shrapnel, but then I guess the only thing that held us together in those B-17s and helped us to get back was our sheer determination to do so.

We didn't get back without losing another thirty bombers, and when we were picked up by the fighter escort on the return trip home, we saw the squadron lose three of their aircraft defending us.

It was the worst mission I'd ever been on, but the irony of it all was that in our debriefing session, we were told that we'd missed the target and had inflicted only minimum damage. The mission had to be done all over again.

By the spring of 1943, the top brass knew that mountainous obstacles confronted us. We had proved we could hit the Germans in daylight and come home, but we were painfully aware of our losses and the slowness of replacing the men and the B-17s. Nonetheless, we went on slugging it out with the Luftwaffe. The place names of targets began to have a familiar ring, as the briefing officers repeated them regularly. Abbeville, Amiens, Antwerp, Amsterdam, Bremen, Saint-Nazaire, Wilhelmshaven, and Schweinfurt. The list and the days grew longer.

Many line chiefs and their mechanics had an almost fanatical concern about the aircraft in their charge. It was often wondered whether they or the actual aircrews had the greatest interest in the B-17s, especially on the return of the big birds. As soon as the engines of the first bomber faltered through the air, everybody turned out to count them in. As each ground crew recognized their own aircraft, the sighs of relief were clearly audible, especially after a long mission.

No matter what the time, the return marked the zenith in each operational day. Excitement grew as one after another touched down, sometimes with very visible damage. The fever pitch was reached as the mechanics and sheet-metal men gave vent to their relief by actually cursing the crew and the damage.

"Sarge, that goddam lieutenant has done it again; there's a hole in her big enough to drive a goddam jeep through."

Lost in the heat of the moment was the fact that the lieutenant in question had also brought back two badly wounded crew members as well as their beloved plane.

That was nothing compared to the atmosphere prevailing when their plane did not fly home at all. They were utterly dejected and indescribably frustrated.

I guess I made every mistake in the book when it came to social manners in the United Kingdom. To begin with, I was always hungry and sometimes thought I could hear my stomach growling even over the roar of the engines. The mess hall was under the control of the Royal Air Force, and we ate what they ate, except that we didn't. When I first arrived and saw all the meat, I thought, *Oh boy! Am I gonna like it here!* But the one and only meat they served was mutton, and I couldn't even put it on my fork, let alone swallow it. Most of the time I ate K rations or bread and butter and jam. But a hungry soldier can't live by bread alone, and whenever I got off base, I'd run for the nearest restaurant or pub, looking for something good to eat.

One day, Jeremy and I and a couple of our other crew members went into Bedford and headed straight to the Brasserie, since we were told they had really good food. We picked out our table by the window, and a lovely young waitress came over and asked what we desired.

"This is only a limited menu," she explained. "The war, you know. But I'd recommend the Welsh rarebit."

I didn't like rabbit too much, but I was practically starving, and since she said it was the best dinner they had, we asked for four orders, well done. As a matter of fact, I hadn't tasted it, but I liked it a lot, hoping there would be enough to go around. In any case, the waitress returned with four little plates; we looked down at them and thought they actually looked like melted cheese on toast.

"Well, let's dig in, boys," I said, and we ate it in record time, thinking it was just an appetizer before the main course would arrive. We waited for what seemed like an hour, but the waitress never came back to our table. We finally called her over, and I said, "We're still waiting, miss, for our rabbit."

"That was it!" she declared. "You've just eaten it."

"But that was only melted cheese on toast," I said, feeling a blush start to creep up from my neck and spread over my cheeks.

"And that's what Welsh rarebit is," she replied. "Melted cheese on toast! You didn't think I said rabbit, did you? Oh, you Yanks are incredible!"

When she walked away, we got our money out and paid the bill, leaving the restaurant feeling as foolish as teenagers on their first date. But by the time we got outside on the sidewalk, we started laughing at one another so hard that our stomachs hurt. Even though people turned to look at us and muttered under their breath, we just kept laughing until we couldn't laugh anymore.

We were all still hungry, so we stopped for our first taste of fish and chips, ordering two apiece, and we ended up throwing the fish away and filling up on the greasy chips. Our next stop was the pub, since we were all ready to get stinking drunk, and hopefully we would meet some nice young ladies to keep us company. As it turned out, there were ten women in England for every man, since so many of their men were away fighting in Africa and elsewhere.

We didn't know much about English beer except that we didn't like to drink it at room temperature, and when I asked the bartender if he had any beer on ice, he said, "If I 'ad any, which I don't, I wouldn't put good beer in it, mate, since it would be a sin to water it down."

It didn't take too long or too many beers for us to start liking it and to start liking anything and everything we saw.

Around five o'clock, when the shops along the street were closing, the girls began to come in. Jeremy and I were soon joined by two Irish lassies named Maureen and Birdy.

"So, you're Americans," Maureen said to me.

I nodded. Then, for some reason, I said, "No, to be exact, I'm an American, but he"—I pointed to Jeremy—"is a New Yorker, and it makes all the difference in the world."

"What do you mean, Vergara?" he said, punching me gently on the shoulder. "He's only kidding around, girls." Jeremy turned to see whether they understood we were only joking. "After all, any New Yorker would be happy to admit that the rest of the country belongs to the United States too."

We started laughing all over again, getting a little giddy, but the girls joined in, and by the time the bartender told us we had five minutes to order our last drink, we were all getting along so well that the girls wanted to buy us a round.

I went up to the bar with Maureen to help her carry the glasses, but there was such a crowd standing there that she had to elbow her way through them. Some Scotsmen were standing in front of us, and they reluctantly let us through.

Maureen decided to order four full pints, since they would be the last drinks for the evening, and I signaled for Jeremy to come over and help me. While we were waiting, one of the Scottish soldiers put his hand on my shoulder and said, in a very harsh tone of voice, and loud enough for everyone to hear him, "Gentlemen do not buy pints of beer for ladies, not in this country. But what can you expect from a Yank?"

I didn't get it. If you were a gentleman, then why wouldn't you buy a lady a beer? I was really insulted, but before I had a chance to say anything, Maureen cut in and told the Scottie to mind his own bloody business.

"I'm not talking to you, lass," he told her. "I'm talking to the bloody Yank!"

Well, that really made me angry, so I grabbed him by the collar, but before I could take a swing at him, he beat me to it. I saw it coming, so

I ducked, but he kept right on through with his swing and hit Maureen clean in the jaw. She went down, out cold.

Then there were three other Scots standing right in front of me, and by the looks of them, they really meant business. I felt someone grab me by the right shoulder. It was Jeremy to the rescue. He pulled me out of the crowd by climbing three short steps into the doorway of the next room.

Suddenly we were standing face-to-face with a crowd of angry civilian drunks, not just the three Scots, all of them raring to get their hands on us. I don't know whose idea it was, Jeremy's or mine, but we all at once decided to try an old football trick on the whole crowd, and luckily for us, it worked like a charm. We joined hands and rushed them like blockers, hitting them with such force that they staggered on top of one another, falling down the three steps and landing in a heap, giving us time to get out of the pub before the MPs arrived.

We learned a lesson that night. You don't buy beer for ladies in pint-size glasses. I knew I would never do it again, whatever the reason was.

I felt terrible for Maureen because she had taken the brunt of that soldier's walloping punch right on the jaw, and it had been meant for me. When I saw her a week later at another pub, I went up to her to apologize, almost hoping that she wouldn't recognize me.

"I'm really sorry about what happened the other night," I said to her, taking my hat off and trying to think of more to say that would make her feel better.

She squinted at me, as if she were wondering who I was, but then it seemed to dawn on her, and she replied, "Oh, I'm all right, Jack. Where's your little friend?"

I turned around and pointed to a corner table. "He's over there, and the name is Mark, not Jack. Can we buy you a drink tonight? Anything you like, as long as it's not a pint."

"That's very kind of you, I'm sure," she answered, hesitating for a moment. "I'm with a friend. Her name is Betty, and she must be around here somewhere. Maybe she's powdering her nose. Wait until she comes back, then we'll join you if you like. Okay, mate?"

"That'll be fine with us," I told her, looking forward to the female companionship. It took me a few minutes to get back to our table, since the pub was very crowded that night. I liked it that way, though. After a few beers, the noise of the laughter and the smoke from cigarettes in the air felt good to me, especially after being on a mission earlier that day.

The people seemed really happy that night, singing to cheer themselves up, and I had the feeling that I could lose myself in the crowd by sitting with my back against the wall, leaning my head back, and listening.

It felt good to be in a crowded roomful of people. I couldn't understand or really hear what they were saying, only catching snatches of their conversations, with laughter and shouting rising in the background from time to time like an orchestration of musical instruments.

Jeremy and I knew each other pretty well, just from having been together for so many months, so I didn't feel that I needed to talk with him. We didn't have to entertain each other; it was just good to be together, away from the barracks and all those empty beds. Whatever was happening in the pub, we were both enjoying it.

When I caught my first glimpse of Betty, I automatically looked over to Jeremy to see if he had noticed her too, but he was looking in another direction, and in that moment, in that split second, I said to myself, *She's mine, and I love her already.*

I made up my mind very quickly, even though I had not yet met her formally. I knew it had to be fate. She filled every image I had ever had of the perfect woman. That was it. I never even knew I had a picture of her in my mind, but all the pieces suddenly seemed to fit, coming together in this one woman. She was about five foot six, with light blond hair and a little V-shaped chin. She had the prettiest smile I'd ever seen. I'd seen pretty smiles before, but hers was so sincere and happy, and she was suddenly looking straight at me. It gave me the impression that I was the one who was making her smile that way.

*She loves me too!* I thought, and by this time I was sitting straight and had already hand combed my hair and straightened the knot in my tie, without even thinking about doing it first.

She was wearing a dark blue suit that almost looked as if it were a uniform. She had a little hat on, with flowers on top. I never took my eyes off her the whole time she was crossing the room with Maureen to get to our table. Sometimes she had to raise her glass over her head and the heads of the people around her to avoid spilling her shandy, and as corny as it sounds, she reminded me of the Statue of Liberty, holding the torch, the emblem of what it meant to live freely and happily in her homeland. The symbol of English public life was being free to drink with your friends and sing a song of sixpence, if you felt like it, with no one telling you who was allowed to be there and who wasn't.

I suddenly felt hot and knew I was madly in love, and we hadn't even spoken yet. I knocked on the table to get Jeremy's attention, then pulled his hand. "Jeremy, there's the girl. There she is," I said to him, as she and Maureen were approaching our table.

"What girl?" Jeremy asked, looking around the crowded pub. "What are you talking about?"

"The girl I'm going to marry. That's what girl!"

Jeremy snickered and shrugged his shoulders. "You're nuts, Vergara. That's what you are!"

The girls were getting closer and closer, but it was as if they were walking in slow motion, almost underwater, and Jeremy had the time to say, "What if she's already married?" before they could move another step forward.

"Married? She's not married. If she is, she'll just have to get a divorce. She can't be married, Jeremy; she has been waiting for me all these years."

"Now I know you are nuts, Mark," my best friend said, and we both stood up at the exact same moment as my future wife was finally standing in front of me.

# CHAPTER SEVEN

POOR MAUREEN had a nasty-looking purple and yellow bruise on her face where she had been hit, taking the punch that had been meant for me, so I felt especially grateful and tender about her, as if she were my sister. I used the opportunity to show off in front of Betty, to show her what a gentleman I really was.

"Gee, I hope you're not too sore at me," I said to her as she and Betty sat down. Jeremy had to move his chair over a bit to keep our knees from bumping into theirs, but I hoped Betty wouldn't mind if we were seated close to each other. I kept turning to look at her, but I kept talking, like a fool, to Maureen.

"You look terrible, Maureen. I mean, the stain on your face looks awful. I mean you look fine, but you really must have been in pain!"

"I feel fine, Mark," she said with a laugh. "Never mind about my face looking so terrible."

"I guess you want to punch me in the nose, huh?"

"Yeah, and you deserve it," Jeremy butted in, poking me in the ribs as we all started laughing.

Betty hadn't said anything. She was just watching me, as if she were waiting to see how she'd like me. I didn't know what to say to her. It made me feel like I was a high school kid again, when the girls would stare at us as we played baseball, with their fingers hooked inside the school-yard fence, and we would show off a lot more than we normally did when we were alone.

I couldn't do anything right, even as I asked Maureen to accept my apologies. I bowed at the waist and almost bumped my head on the table. I was just a barrel of laughs, and everyone was having a really good time, or so I thought. Betty whispered something to Maureen and got up, finishing off her drink. Then she left.

*She can't just get up and leave like that*, I thought. *She can't walk into my life and then walk straight out of it again, without even saying a word to me.* But she had.

"What's wrong?" I asked Maureen. "Did I say something wrong? Is she coming back again?"

"Hold on, mate," Maureen said, patting my arm. "She's got to get to work. She's late, that's all. Betty works at the Plaza Movie Theatre. She's an usherette there, just like me."

"Well, then let's all go to the movies. How about it, Jeremy?" I looked at my buddy as I stood up, ready to make a beeline for the Plaza.

"What's your hurry, Mark?" Jeremy replied. "Sit down, old boy. We just got here."

"But I—but I—" I started to say, as he pulled me down into my chair. "Aw, now I'll never see her again, and she's . . . Well, I just have to see her again, that's all!"

Jeremy and Maureen were laughing at me. Poking fun at me and saying, "Aw, the boy is in love."

"You certainly didn't act like you wanted to see her," Maureen said with a smile. "You kept talking to me the whole time she was here. You never even asked her the time of day!"

"Why would I need to ask her the time of day? I know what time it is." They both laughed some more.

"Listen, don't feel bad, Mark. If you like, I'll take you to the Corn Exchange. It's a big dance hall in Bedford, with an excellent band. They play all the new American tunes like Benny Goodman and Glenn Miller. Do you like to dance?" Maureen looked at me, holding her hand up over her purple-and-yellow-bruised eye and face.

"I love to dance," I told her. "Will Betty be there later?"

"She may come over there after work, but there are plenty of girls to dance with in town. You can have the pick of the lot if you are a good dancer. So, how's about it? Are you both game?"

I turned to Jeremy, who said, "Sure, I'm game. Let's go."

I suddenly felt foolish for feeling so bad about Betty, thinking that I'd never see her again, but I missed her already, as if a part of me had been torn right out. I'd always been a good dancer, so I said, "What the hell, sure, let's go and dance our heads off."

When we got outside, Jeremy and I walked on either side of Maureen. Jeremy was acting up, joking around like he always did.

"We're not all as funny as Mark, Maureen. You see, he comes from the sunny Southwest, so his brain is fried. Now, on the other hand, I come from New York, so I'm smarter and funnier and more handsome than Mark will ever be. Naturally."

"Naturally!" Maureen was shaking with laughter and put her arm through Jeremy's. She said it was nice for her to walk with a smart and funny and handsome Yank on each arm. She was smiling so much that I could finally forget about the bruise on her face, as if my debt to her had been paid in full.

The dance hall had an eight-piece band, and there were plenty of girls to go around, some of them even doing the jitterbug, which was one of my favorites. I stood back, watching the girls to see which ones would be good partners. Jeremy was doing fine, dancing with the same brunette, whether it was a slow dance or a fast one, but always in the same way, holding her very close to him and moving slowly back and forth. They glided across the floor together as if they had known each other for years.

I finally started to dance and never stopped, except when the band took a break. Then I spotted this pretty girl and asked her if she would dance with me, but she was all out of breath, resting at a table, and she said, "I'm sorry. I can't just now. I'm all knocked up. But thank you very much."

I was stunned. My mouth fell open and I just stood there, gawking at her. She must have thought I was an idiot, but I wondered, if she was knocked up, what was she doing at a dance hall, and why had she told me she was pregnant?

I walked back to my spot by the door, very much in a daze and deep in thought. I kept looking over at her, and since she didn't seem to be sitting with any particular man, I thought maybe being pregnant and unmarried might be all right in England.

A few minutes later, I made the mistake of asking a British soldier about it, which only made things worse.

"Oh yes," he said. "You see, they dance ever so much that they become knocked up, and then they stop for a while. That only makes sense, doesn't it?"

*That's stupid*, I thought. *Girls can't get pregnant by dancing. Someone is pulling a fast one on me.*

I couldn't take the suspense any longer. I went back up to the girl and asked her to dance a slow dance with me. We didn't talk for a while, and as I held her tightly against my chest, I kept trying to see if I could feel her pregnancy. She finally looked up at me and spoke.

"I'm sorry I didn't dance with you the first time you asked, but I was really out of it."

*Out of what?* I thought. *Out of breath?*

She was a good dancer. As we glided together, I tried to relax with her in my arms, but it felt so strange that I finally pushed back a little and asked, "Is your husband here with you tonight?"

She stopped in her tracks and looked up at me, still holding my hand. "No, I'm not married. Whatever gave you that idea?"

I could feel the fingers of her other hand tightening up at the back of my neck. "Not married?" I said to her. "But you told me you were pregnant before, when I asked you to dance the first time." We were both standing stock-still in the middle of the dance floor.

"I did no such thing!" she exclaimed, pulling her hands away from me.

"But you said you were knocked up, didn't you?" I asked her in a strong and demanding tone of voice.

"Yes, I said that, and knocked up, for your information, means *tired* over here, you nut! Tired, worn-out, that's what it means to be knocked up in England!"

"Well, in the States it means that you are pregnant, for God's sake!" I shouted, with everyone turning around to look and laugh at me.

"But you are not in the States, Yank. We say and do things differently over here, mate," my partner said, putting her hands down on her knees to keep herself from falling over; that's how hard she was laughing.

"Hey, the next time you dance with a Yank," I replied, "you'd better not tell him how knocked up you are, whether you're knocked up or not." And with that, I turned around and left the dance, wondering if I would ever learn to understand the British way of saying and doing things.

I went back to the barracks and thought about Betty. I carried a picture of her in my mind wherever I went and whatever I did. She was always in my thoughts. I'd never had a woman's attraction strike me so deeply or so hard. I wanted to go to town and find her again, but the springtime weather was so good in England, we were all put on alert and confined to base. We were doing one mission after another; to Rouen, Amiens, Vegesack, Lorient, and Saint-Nazaire again.

Our morale was low, and our losses were heavy. Replacements were coming into the barracks, but only a few of us got to know them. Some we never got to know at all, not their names or where they were from, whether they were married, or anything else about them. When the mattresses were rolled up, exposing the bedsprings, we knew they would have to be replaced again.

Jeremy and I spent our free time at the base canteen, and when our Red Cross director, Nancy Ellsmore, decided to throw a party for us there, she went all out, sending two six-by-six trucks into town to pick up some girls. We couldn't figure out why she was suddenly being so generous to us, or even how she'd gotten permission for the women to come onto the base, but we'd been fighting harder than ever for the past few weeks, so we all decided she had pulled a few strings for us, letting us have some fun, before they sent us out again.

We were told that liquor was absolutely prohibited that night, and of course, we'd gone ahead and poured a couple of bottles of booze in the punch without Nancy knowing it. We called it ball turret punch because some guys had actually gone and got a ball turret from one of our B-17s that was out of commission and set it up in the canteen for the awful-tasting punch that Nancy had made for us. Of course, after the booze was put into it, the stuff didn't taste too bad, and I'm sure there had to be a few more bottles added later in the evening because it ended up tasting better and better and packed quite a wallop in the end.

Nancy had more than her share of the rummed-up punch, and she danced a lot that night. By the time I caught up with her, we were both shaky on our feet and kind of holding on to each other in the doorway to keep ourselves standing up.

"Say, where is everybody?" she asked me, and I put my arm around her waist to help her stand up.

"All gone," I told her, staring out into the dark night, wondering how the hell I was going to get her to her quarters. Then I realized she was crying. She swooned around a bit, landing her head on mine suddenly, the way a bomber might come down on an airfield without approaching it just right, bumping and jerking, then sliding the rest of the way before coming to a halt.

"What'za matter, Nancy?" I asked her.

"All gone," she answered, repeating my earlier words. "They're all gone now, brothers, fathers, uncles, and nephews. All the fine young men are gone now, and the husbands too!"

"Oh my God," I said, realizing that she had lost someone very close to her, although I didn't dare ask whether it was her husband.

I decided to walk around with her a bit, to help her clear her head, and she didn't protest when I lifted her head from my shoulder and draped her arm through mine. I started to lead her down the pathway that led around the little square near the canteen, and either she was too drunk or too tired or too unhappy to notice what I was seeing as my eyes became accustomed to the darkness.

There were people lying everywhere, couples, on the grass and on the benches, with their arms around each other so closely that it was hard to tell where one ended and the other began.

I started to walk a little more quickly to make sure Nancy wouldn't notice the couples making love, since I thought it would break her heart to see it, especially if it was really her husband who had been killed. I led her to her quarters, making sure she got in all right before I said good-bye.

"All the fine young men," she whispered to me, and then closed the door.

As I walked back to my barrack, I didn't feel so drunk anymore, but there was plenty more to drink when I stepped inside, and then I realized where a lot of the girls had disappeared to. I turned the lights on—it was a natural habit—and someone shouted to douse the lights. In the second it took me to turn the lights off again, I saw something I'd never seen before. They were there in the barracks with the men, and some of them were as naked as jaybirds.

I went around to all the bunks, but they all had two people in them. I disturbed one couple getting a good peek.

"Hey! Get outta here!" Wiznewsky said as I lifted up the blanket.

*Sweet Jesus*, I thought. *What a war.* Then I found a bottle of scotch and poured myself a drink.

"Can I have one too?" someone asked, definitely a feminine voice.

I couldn't see where it was coming from, but I strained my eyes and then said, "Sure, but you gotta come and get it yourself."

"Okay, soldier." And she did just that, walking right up and sitting down beside me.

"Jesus, Mary, and Joseph!" I said in disbelief. And no sooner had I said it than two more naked girls were sitting next to me on my bunk. If the MPs hadn't thrown open the doors at that very minute, I might have had the most enjoyable night of my entire life.

People were scrambling all over the place, and one of the girls said to me, "I'm small enough to hide beneath you, so lie down on top of me, and they might not see me. All right?"

"Sure," I told her, "sure, I won't mind a bit," realizing that the other women had run to get their clothes on.

She got into the bed, and I quickly lay down on top of her, throwing the blanket over me and trying as hard as I could not to move around too much, hoping I would not smother her in the process. She was lying facedown, and I could feel the curve of her back under me. That's not all I could feel, and I held my breath, hoping the MPs wouldn't find her, because I was thinking that maybe, after they left, I could relieve myself of the growing urge I now felt. Lying there on top of her, my urge was feeling stronger and stronger all the time.

It didn't work out that way. As it happened, the night ended with a bang, but not the kind of bang I'd been hoping for. As the MPs started tearing through the barracks, making everyone get up from their cots, someone had the smart idea to take some unspent ammo and throw it into the potbellied stove in the middle of the room. I'd seen fireworks before, but never up so close.

The whole stove started glowing like a furnace; someone was smart enough and fast enough to yell, "Everyone get the hell out—the stove's gonna blow!"

We all made it in the nick of time, running like madmen out the door, half dressed or still completely undressed, and then it blew all right, blowing out most of the windows in the barracks and half the roof off.

Thank God we were all still alive. It would have been too ironic if we had died that way, naked and drunk and some of us making love, as if there weren't any war going on. For the first time in weeks, we were all just the happiest of men, having the time of our lives on a Saturday night.

We might have made a lot of noise that night, but our morale was still low, and it got worse with every new mission we flew. We were all feeling sorry for ourselves, and our group commander thought it was time to give us a pep talk.

He called us in to the briefing room and then let the little intelligence officer tell us that we had to keep bombing those submarine pens since our mail was not getting through, and we needed our mail to keep our morale high! Who the hell cared about the mail? we mumbled. We didn't, and we were the ones who had to bomb the goddam submarine pens, not the guy of little intelligence!

There were more fatalities in our squadron than any other, and even our commander, who'd been with us since Wendover, Utah, was beginning to call us a hard-luck group. But when he was replaced with a new commanding officer, we weren't allowed to feel sorry for ourselves anymore. We were called in for another morale talk and to meet the new commander. We found out soon enough that he meant what he said.

"I know how it's been for you," he told us. "You come back from a mission, and half of your friends are still lying out there somewhere in the ocean or on a piece of farmland or in the hospital with their lives blown half out of them. But that gives us even more of a reason to go on fighting.

"I also know, in the beginning, that at the end of a mission, you'd rush to find out who'd been killed, so you could run into their barracks and go through their stuff, taking almost everything that was left of those dead men. But you don't do that anymore, do you? Do you?" he asked again, in such a loud and sharp tone of voice that we all snapped to attention.

"So maybe some of you don't want to fly anymore. At least that's all I've been hearing since I got here. So if there is anyone who wants to quit now, just stand up!"

We looked around the room, certain there would be at least four or five guys who'd stand up, since they had been the most unhappy of the lot. No one stood up. The room grew as silent as a tomb.

Then the general said it again, only this time he made it sound more ominous. "If there's anyone in this room right now with a yellow stripe down his back, then let him stand up and show his face to me. I dare you!"

*I'd rather be killed*, I thought. *I'd rather die the most horrible death in the world than have someone even think I have a yellow stripe down my back. And you—you son of a bitch—you know that none of us will do it, no matter how much we suffer on the goddam missions.*

The commander went on with his speech. "Well, that's just fine, now, isn't it? I see we have no yellow dogs in this group. But then maybe someone can tell me what the hell is the matter with this damned organization!" He waited for someone to answer him, knowing that no one would say a word. "Well, if no one's going to tell me what's wrong with you, then I'll just have to find out for myself, I guess."

I could see our old commander squirming in his chair.

"From this day on, if you are not flying a mission over enemy territory, then you'll be flying training missions over East Anglia. Then you won't have any more time to sit around and feel sorry for yourselves or go into town to cry in your beer. Therefore, all passes will be canceled until further notice. That's all for now."

Then the adjutant gave the command, "Attention!"

After everyone stood as the general left the room, the first sergeant shouted out, "Dismissed!"

That was the end of our good times, and whatever morale we had left flew right back to the States with our old commanding officer, whom we never saw again.

# CHAPTER EIGHT

WE HAD A FEW good times after that, but we could count them on our fingers. One morning the combat crews were called into the dayroom and surprised by the news that we were being issued bicycles, one for each of us, courtesy of His Majesty, the King of England. Well, that was nice, and we were all very happy to have some kind of transportation. But the ground crews weren't given any bicycles, and the bikes started disappearing all over the place. One night after Jeremy and I had ridden them into town, we parked our bikes behind the pub where all the others were parked. By the time we had hitched a ride back to the barracks on a truck, Jeremy said, "Hey! We forgot the damned bikes!"

"Did we leave them behind the pub?" I asked.

"Yea, but which pub was it?" Jeremy replied.

"It had to be the Rod and Reel," I told him.

In any case, having them was beginning to feel like taking an umbrella out on a rainy day. When you needed it, it was fine, but after you had parked it somewhere, who the hell cared or remembered where and when and what the hell he had done with it? Well, the Army cared, that's who, since it wouldn't look good if the king ever found out that his presents weren't being cared for in the good old English way. Every night, a truck full of MPs was sent into town to round up all the bikes that had been left behind the pubs.

I wouldn't have mentioned the bikes, except that I was glad I had one after one of the most decisive bombing runs into Germany. It was the one mission I didn't go out on, since I'd come down with double pneumonia. I had a fever of 105, and I was put into the infirmary for eight days. By the time I got out, I found out that my crew had all died, every single one of them.

Someone should have told me about them while I was still in bed, because then I could have mourned for them, even weeping to get the shock and sorrow out of my stomach. I could have rolled over and bit my lip and closed my eyes from the pain I felt, and I could have prayed for them. I could have sat in bed and written a letter to Jeremy's parents, but now I had to tell myself that I'd do it tomorrow because I was back in the barracks, sleeping with new men all around me.

I was told that since I had lost my crew I'd have to float around from then on, going up with a different plane every day. I said, "Oh, in that case, I'll just check in for my orders every day. Is that right?"

"That's right," the adjutant answered. "I'm sorry."

"Sure," I said, "I'm sorry too."

I walked over to where the bicycles were kept, took one, and started riding it, slowly at first, then faster and faster around the base like a crazy man, with the wind whistling in my ears. I didn't stop for the longest time, not even when it started raining, rushing through it like someone on his way to a funeral, pumping my legs so fast and hard that they began to ache and stiffen up and then turned so numb that I couldn't feel them moving anymore.

I fell off the damned thing and lay in a puddle with the rain splashing all over me, and I started kicking my legs on the ground and pounding my fists into the water. I heard myself cry out, "It isn't fair! It just isn't fair!" over and over again, until it didn't seem to matter anymore.

I could have died right there from a relapse of the pneumonia, from drowning with my face in the puddle of water, or from being so crazy with grief and bitterness. I guess it wasn't that easy to die, not for me, not when I wanted to, not from begging God to put an end to my misery.

"They should have waited for me!" I said to the trees, to the mud, to the sad and rippling reflection of my face in the water. They hadn't waited; they'd gone off on their damned mission without me, and I was the only one left to remember them.

I didn't talk much to the guys anymore, the ones who were still left. I didn't make new friends, keeping to myself as much as I could, even mumbling to myself under my breath like a crazy man.

I'd been like a dead man for about a month, in sympathy for my pals, but I couldn't live that way forever. When they sent me on one mission after another, I was soon brought back to my senses again. My whole body would become alert and ready to react at a moment's notice.

I watched and listened and felt every movement of the plane's body, since it was my life-support system. I was breathing again, even smiling once in a while. Every time we set the plane down on base and walked out onto the ground, I thanked God. Alive, to fight another day, that's all that mattered to me then.

I was awarded the Distinguished Flying Cross and another oak leaf cluster for successfully completing my twentieth mission. After the little ceremony, I went into town with a very quiet kid named Bobby Rosemont. He was a crew survivor, like me. Even though he didn't say much to me, I knew he'd be there when I needed him, as I would him.

We had been given a three-day pass and decided to go into London and really live it up. We walked into the Rod and Reel for two fifths of scotch to bring on the train to London. Maureen came right over to me, shaking my hand and saying, "Welcome back, mate! We heard all about your last run over Germany on the wireless."

Then everyone was raising their glasses in our honor, and the landlord held up a newspaper to show us the headlines, which read: YANKS KEEP THE NAZIS ON THE RUN. GOD BLESS THE YANKS.

As we smiled and nodded to the people who were toasting our good health, I saw Betty at the same corner table where I'd first met her. She raised her glass, and I nodded. "Excuse me a minute," I said to Bobby. "I have to do something." She wasn't even mine yet, but I knew I wanted her.

"May I?" I asked, pointing to the empty chair.

"Yes, please, sit down," she said, looking shyly into her lap. "Are you all right? I mean, well, you have been on a lot of missions lately, haven't you?"

"I'm fine, thank you. We're going into London; would you like to come with us?" I knew she would say no, but I had to ask her.

"Oh, no, thank you," she answered, "but I couldn't. You do have a lot to celebrate, don't you?"

"Celebrate?" I asked, remembering the boys in my crew who couldn't come with us. "No, well, that is, yes. I've got a whole lot of celebrating to do for some good friends of mine. They couldn't make it this time around."

"Have they been restricted?" she politely asked. Then she laughed a little, as if she was talking about some child that had been naughty.

"Yes, you could say that. Well, I have to be going now, but I'd like to see you again," I said very quietly. "May I call you? Maybe we can get together sometime, when I'm not celebrating."

"Yes, if you like. I'll give you my telephone number. It's my grandparents' number really. I live with them, and they wouldn't mind if I saw you. I already asked them, you see."

"You've told them about me? They know who I am?"

"Oh, yes," she said, grinning. "I could hardly keep you a secret all to myself, now, could I?"

I didn't really know what she meant by that, but it didn't matter. She had told them about me, and they had already given their permission for her to see me! Maybe she had gone out with a lot of men, but I didn't think so. I didn't think she would have told her grandparents about me unless she really cared for me.

I got up, and as I reached out to shake her hand good-bye, she stood up and kissed me on the cheek.

"You're such a dear," she said. "Go on, now. Don't miss your train; you deserve a night in London."

At that moment, London was the furthest thing from my mind. She had written her name on a small card before giving it to me. I promised to call her after I got back from London.

As I settled in my seat on the train, I took my wallet out to look at her name. Eliza Betty Bishop, a good name. I imagined all kinds of things during the next two hours, staring out the window and watching the scenery go by.

When we arrived in London, someone suggested we all go to the Eagle Club, which had been founded by members of the famous Eagle Squadrons of the RAF, but it was now an all-American club. These Americans had come over at the beginning of the war in 1939 to join the RAF, and they'd seen service all over the world. It was the best place for us to get haircuts and have our shoes shined and our uniforms pressed.

Ready for a night on the town, we went to the Strand Palace Hotel, and as we entered the large dining room, people started applauding us. I looked over my shoulder a few times, to see if anyone famous was standing there, but Bobby pointed to my wings and ribbons, and he said, "They mean us! They're clapping for us, Mark!"

Everyone was talking about the daring daylight raids over Germany, and as the maître d' escorted us to a table, people were stopping us, saying things like, "You're doing a bang-up job, Yanks! Good show, Captain!"

Somebody sent over free drinks, then someone else did the same, so we nodded at them, raised our glasses in good cheer, and glowed in our quiet pride.

After about an hour, I stood up, feeling no pain from the steady flow of free drinks, and I said, in a somewhat shaky voice, "I propose a toast, to all the missing, the dead, and the dying!" Then I sat down, and the room grew very quiet. But before long another man was standing, and then another, and then we all stood up and toasted the dead and the dying, since they were maybe the greatest heroes of this war.

Bobby and I went to the theater that night, and we decided to buy the most expensive seats available. "What the hell, let's live it up," Bobby said. I was more than willing to spend every penny that I had, since there didn't seem much sense in saving it.

During the intermission, when the lights came up, the master of ceremonies came onstage, lifted his hand in our direction, and said, "Ladies and gentlemen, let's have a round of applause for our allies, the Americans. God bless them and support them in accomplishing their missions!"

Oh, it was heady stuff, a real ego builder, the stuff that dreams are made of, especially when the free bottle of champagne arrived with two glasses. Bobby and I suddenly felt as though we had accomplished every mission single-handed. I know I felt that every minute of being chased and shot at by the Germans had been worth it, reaching this moment of appreciation and gratitude from the English people.

I was also beginning to feel very dizzy, giddy, as if I were about to fall. I woke up at someone's house, a girl named Connie whom I'd apparently met at the New Havana Club. You had to be a member to go in there, but I didn't remember how I'd gotten there, let alone who invited me.

Bobby was in the house too, so I must have been with him when we picked up the girls. There were girls and other Americans too, lying all around the house, everywhere I looked. *I must have had a pretty good time*, I said to myself. I still had all my clothes on, so I assumed that I'd acted like a gentleman before I passed out.

It was one o'clock in the afternoon; I had lost all track of time between those glasses of champagne at the theater and now. It didn't matter really, except that this girl Connie came up to me as I sat in the kitchen rubbing my eyes.

"You sure were swell to me last night, dearie," she said, kissing my cheek and licking the back of my neck.

"Hey, wait a minute!" I said, pulling away from her. "Not so fast, huh?"

"Not so fast?" she quickly blurted out. "Not so fast? You were fast enough last night; I'll say that much for you!"

"I was? Well, I don't remember. It's all a blur to me now. What did I do, and what did you say your name was?"

"Connie," she replied, laughing. "Don't you remember anything?"

I just shook my head, trying to get the cobwebs out of it. I noticed she had bare feet. Somehow her feet seemed so funny to me; I mean, she was all dressed up except for her feet, and I guess I broke out laughing. She spun around and glared at me, and then I realized I must have been in her house.

I didn't know what I had done to this girl, but it must have been very intimate by the way she spoke to me. She certainly wouldn't have licked my neck if we had not gotten close the night before.

"We met at the Havana Club, remember? We started dancing, and all the while you kept telling me how much you liked Latin music. I called you my Latin lover—that was cute, wasn't it? But you were cute last night, and so was I."

She smiled and closed her eyes, remembering the dancing with a sigh. "Do you remember the blokes from the Eagle Squadron showing up?" she asked me. "Well, there was this big man from Texas, and he got into a terrible row with one of them, and they took their fight outside the club. You jumped up from the table, taking me and Bob along with you. By the time we got there, it was all over, and then the door-man wouldn't let us back inside. To top it all off, the air-raid warning went off, so you banged on the door of the club until the doorman finally understood that we were in danger.

"We stayed until the sun came up, and then we all came over here to my parents' house. And here we are, love, just you and me in the kitchen, and this nice cup of tea I've just made for you."

I remembered the Texan singing "Deep in the Heart of Texas," and I picked up the tune where he had left off, but when Connie brought me the tea, sat down across from me, and told me the story of what happened during the night and early morning, I didn't remember any of it. I must have had an awfully good time from the way she described it all.

I wanted to stay friendly with this girl because I liked being able to come to her house with a bunch of guys and sow a few wild oats before I settled down. I knew I could never have done this with Betty because she was different. I made a date to see Connie again in two weeks, if we were still alive. Then I found Bobby in a pile of people, helped him out of the arms and legs that were flung over him, and we went back to the Strand Hotel to settle our bill.

It seemed a shame to have a room that we didn't even use, and it was a shame that I didn't remember how good a time I'd had with Connie. That's why I wanted to see her again, if only for one more time, to find out whether I could relive that night so that I'd always remember how much fun she actually was.

On my next pass to London, Bobby and I got so drunk with Connie and her sisters that I started calling Bobby Jeremy and Connie Betty. She threw me out and said she never wanted to see me again. I never did find out just how much of a good time I'd had with her.

I had only three more missions to fly before they would send me home, and I made up my mind that it was senseless to spend what might have been my last days on earth with just any woman. Betty was a really fine girl, honest and saying what she felt without trying to impress me or flatter. I knew she brought out the best in me. She made me feel good about myself whenever I saw her.

*If I could help her get over her shyness*, I thought, *then I might be able to talk her into going with me for my one week's R & R at Southport.*

It was the summer of 1943. Betty didn't like to drink very much, so we would go to dinner dances. I had a whole week's leave coming up, I felt happier than ever, and I wanted her to share my good fortune with me.

We took a stroll after dinner, and I didn't know whether she would let me put my arm around her waist or not. And yet there I was, planning to sweep her off her feet and bring her along with me for a week of lovemaking and sleeping late and staying up all night, if we felt like it. But first I'd have to make my way up from holding her to kissing her and then to getting her in bed.

From the way she kissed me, I knew I was the first one. She may have kissed other guys before, but when I held her in my arms and felt her pressed against me, felt her lips on mine, I knew that she wanted me as much as I wanted her.

When she told me that she never wanted me to go away from her, I knew this was my big break, my chance to get her to come with me.

"Listen, before you say no," I said, "just listen to me for a minute. I want you to stay with me too, forever. Maybe some people think that this is the worst time for us to fall in love, but don't you see? If I'm going to die out there in the skies someday, then I'm going to die whether you come to Southport or not. If you don't come with me, Betty, then you'll have nothing to remember me by. Just this, our dinner dates together. Is that all you want from me?"

"No, Mark. Of course I want more. I want it all. But how will I ever explain it to Nanna?" She looked down at the steps of an old house where we had seated ourselves, not far from where she lived with her grandparents, before she spoke again. "I think my grandpa would understand. He'd probably wink his eye and pat me on the back and send me off with his best wishes. But my nan, well, she is very strict with me. She believes in doing things right. The proper way, like getting married first. I know she wouldn't let me, Mark. And I'm going to start crying now, thinking that you might die someday."

"Well, I don't plan to die. Don't you see? I won't die, Betty. That's an even better reason for you to come with me because when I finish my twenty-fifth mission, then we can get married. Would you like that, Betty?"

"Are you proposing, Mark?"

"Yes. Will you? Marry me, I mean."

"Do you really mean that, Mark?" she asked, looking up at me and taking my hand. "Or are you just saying that to get me to go to Southport with you?"

"I really mean it. We can bring up our children in the New World. That's what my father used to call it. The New World. I'll take you back with me, all the way to Colorado and then California. I'd want to make one stop along the way, though, to visit some people in New York, the parents of a good friend of mine. Then we could take a nice long train ride across the country, and you'd see how great it is. We could go anywhere, Betty, and do anything we wanted to do."

I didn't realize I was offering her somewhat more than I would be able to give her, since I would go where the Army sent me, but I believed what I was saying then, and I meant every word of it, whether it would ever really come true or not. I believed in her.

We kissed for a long time, sitting there on the steps of that old house. Then she said, "I will go with you to Southport, but I won't tell my nanna that I am going with you. I'll just tell her I'm going with a friend. Anyway, I'm almost nineteen, and I guess I can make up my own mind now. Huh?"

"You certainly can!" I said, feeling on top of the world. "It'll be great, you'll see. We'll catch the end of the summer and ride it all the way to paradise!"

I could hardly believe that she'd said yes, even when she was sitting on the train next to me, cuddling up close and leaning her head on my shoulder. But it was real, and I had never known this feeling before, of wanting to protect someone and be her guide, to show her how good life could be, to be her one and only lover in all the world.

I was very possessive of her from the first, wanting to keep her all to myself, wanting her to belong to me. Betty wanted to belong to me too, or maybe I should say we belonged together, to each other. Neither of us felt like a whole person without the other one; we were one together.

She lost her shyness during the week in Southport. We hardly left our hotel room, and it was almost embarrassing to go down to the dining room and eat with all those strangers around us. I had the feeling that everyone knew exactly what we had done together and that our only purpose in life seemed to be to make love to each other.

Betty was just as reserved and polite as she had always been in public, but she became a woman in our hotel room. After making love, we would lie together, sometimes falling asleep holding hands, listening in the dark to the sounds coming up from the street below.

We kept the light turned off during the blackouts, but we had brought a candle with us, and Betty would light it, carrying it over to the bed to look at me, she said, just like the woman Psyche in the Greek myth. I didn't know anything about Greek myths, so I asked her to explain it to me, pulling her over to my side. Then I felt like a child again as I lay in the sweet warmth of our bed, listening to the fairy tale she told me.

"The god Cupid fell in love with Psyche, who was supposed to be the most beautiful woman on earth. Well, she was so beautiful that even Venus, Cupid's mother, was jealous of her. Now she was sentenced to a terrible kind of death, as I remember it, because Venus was so jealous of her. She had to sit alone on top of a hill and wait for this awful serpent to come and eat her up, or something like that.

"But Cupid was so in love with her that he flew down from heaven in the form of a soft wind and took her up to his mansion in the sky. But she never saw him, and he told her that they could be perfectly happy together, as long as she never looked at him. She had to promise she'd never do it. She had to love him without ever seeing his face.

"Psyche was very happy because Cupid was such a great lover, just like you! He would come to her every night, but before the sun rose, he would disappear again. She became so lonely, waiting for him all day without ever seeing him, that she asked him if he would allow her two sisters to come up and visit her. What a mistake! When they came, they had a great time for a while, talking about everybody back on earth. But then they planted the seeds of doubt in her mind. They said things like: 'Maybe he's a terrible serpent who was supposed to come and kill you.' Maybe he was just waiting for the right moment and then he would let her have it!

"So, they talked her into looking at him. She was supposed to kill him, I think, but anyway, she waited for hours after he left her, went into the next room where he was sleeping, and walked up to his bed with a candle in her hand. When she saw him, she fell madly in love, right away, of course. But she had been so afraid that he was actually the serpent that her hand was trembling, and the hot, dripping wax from her candle fell on him and woke him up.

"And then, of course, he knew that she had broken her promise, and it took them many, many years to get back together again."

"Well, I'm glad it ended happily ever after," I said to Betty, as she put the candle down on the bedside table next to me, and I looked at her one more time before I blew the candle out. *Yes*, I thought, this was just what I wanted. I wanted to be her Cupid, or whatever she wanted to call me, and to love her forever and ever, even if it was only until tomorrow.

It would take a lot of red tape and paperwork, belonging to the Army as I did, needing their permission to do anything as drastic as getting married. Betty would also need her grandparents' permission too, and after my feelings of euphoria and happiness, I came down to earth long enough to realize that even though we were both adults, we still had responsibilities to other people in the world.

I couldn't sleep the rest of that night. Breathing slowly and deeply, feeling Betty's head rise and fall against my body, I began to have second thoughts about letting this young, intelligent, beautiful girl marry a man who might die on his next mission. It would hardly be fair to Betty, and I only wanted what was best for her.

In the morning, I asked her if we could leave Southport a day early, to have an extra day to speak to her grandparents. I had to know how they felt about me and what I did for the Army Air Corps and whether they felt it was right for their granddaughter to marry a man she hardly knew.

I worried needlessly. They were the most gracious people I had ever met, and they both realized we were truly in love. They gave us their blessing, and I received permission from my commanding officer to be married as soon as all the paperwork was filed.

We were married in Bedford on August 2, 1943. I was allowed to live off base in a small two-room flat, where we settled in with our few possessions, spending some of the happiest moments in my life.

I had only one more mission to fly. Betty was so nervous the night before the mission that she asked me to hold her until she fell asleep. I would never have told her how I was feeling, but deep down I knew that I had to be strong for her, and she was making me feel the strength in myself that I'd never admitted to having before.

*You crazy man*, I said to myself, listening to the steady rhythm of her breathing. I had been strong ever since I was a boy. I was my father's son, and I could draw on his strength! It had been part of me all those years, through all the hard times out there in the beet fields and in the boxcars and every time a bullet or bomb was near. How did I think I had come this far along, without being a tower of strength?

Tomorrow would be the end of a chapter of my life; I'd lived through it as I'd lived through all the others. I would come out victorious and all in one piece. No more fear for me. I couldn't help thinking about it. *No more fear for me.*

My last mission, to Romilly, France, was practically a milk run, with Spitfires escorting us to keep the FW-190s off our tails. I didn't have to fire a single round of ammunition after leaving England, and when we landed, the crew picked me up and tossed me into a dirty pond as their final good-bye and good-luck send-off to me and Betty. I knew then I was a free man. I'd never have to risk my life again on another mission.

I had a choice of assignment. I could go back to the States now or become a gunnery instructor at the Wash gunnery school. It was a joint project of the Eighth Army Air Force and the British army, near a village called Snettisham in Norfolk. I talked it over with Betty.

"I'd love you to stay over here a little longer, Mark. It would be nice for our baby to be born in England."

"Our baby? We're going to have a baby? Are you really, Betty? Really pregnant?"

"Silly man," she said to me, grinning like the Cheshire cat. "You have enough sisters and nieces to know all about it. There'll be a new Vergara in the world, Mark. A brand new life, from me to you. Wonderful isn't it? I can hardly believe it myself, but we must have known that all the fun we've been having in bed would one day end up giving us a child. Are you happy, Mark?"

"Happy?" I answered her. "It doesn't seem possible that you could keep making me happier and happier. I'm on top of the world!"

It's a holy time for a man to become a father, and I felt the enormous responsibility of it. There were many moments in my life that I remembered with clarity and distinctness, but for Betty, it had to be the moment that Dorothy Maria was born, on our first anniversary, August 2, 1944.

*Pappa*, I said to myself, as if he were standing beside me. *Is that you?* I could almost feel his spirit in the room with me. *It's all right, Pappa. We have a new Vergara in this world. I'll do the right thing by her, so don't worry about me anymore. Rest in peace, my father, because everything is going to be all right now.*

# CHAPTER NINE

JOHN BURROUGHS WROTE, "The dominant impression of the English landscape is repose.... The completeness and composure of this outdoor nature is like a dream. It is like the poise of the tide at its full: every hurt of the world is healed."

Every hurt I had ever felt in my life seemed to have been healed. I was suddenly a contented man in this island of beauty and composure.

I loved to walk through the lush green fields with Betty, holding Dorothy in my arms, as Betty picked wildflowers that would soon adorn our table. My life was complete.

I even loved the history of the Old World, the fact that the churches and old castles dated back hundreds of years, everywhere, all over England.

But I had to leave, not knowing when I would see my wife and child again. I was going home. It was November 1944.

It had been more than two years since I'd left as a raw recruit and a single man with no great experiences to boast about or remember. I was going to spend some time with my mother in Delta, and then go wherever the Army decided to send me until the war ended. I wanted to move to California to find a good job and a new place for me, Betty, and Dorothy to live. I was full of hope when I boarded the *Queen Mary*, and I thought I'd seen everything until we hit a ninety-mile-an-hour gale just outside Liverpool.

Having lived through two years of fighting, I had come to think that nothing could ever be as bad as living through all that, but I was not a natural-born seaman, and the ground seemed to have given way completely under my feet.

Nothing on the ship was standing still. My whole world was rocking to and fro, hour after hour, night after day, and I kept wishing I was up in a plane again, being strafed by fighter planes.

In the end, I had to take it, no matter what was being dished out to me, and I couldn't bargain with God. I was so sick I couldn't even sit down for a few minutes and write to Betty to tell her how green my face was, but I wrote to her every day as soon as I got stateside again.

I had something to do in New York. I had to find Jeremy's parents, if I could, and tell them how I felt about their son. They needed to hear it from me—his best friend—what a brave young man he had been and how he had touched my life, never to be forgotten by me.

I stood waiting at his parents' door. I knew exactly what I was going to say to them. When his father opened the door, I was hardly prepared to see an older version of Jeremy himself, standing right in front of me.

"Yes?" asked the man. "Can I help you?"

I was speechless, but he could tell, from my uniform I suppose, why I had come.

"Come in, young man," he said. "You must be Mark. Jeremy wrote us about you, and I just knew that you'd come one day."

He ushered me into his living room and let me look through a family photo album at the pictures of Jeremy and his brother as boys. His brother was in Italy at the time, and I hoped that at least he would survive the war, for his parents' sake.

"I, uh, I didn't know him very long," I told his father, "but I knew him very well. He brought out the best in me; that's why I liked him most of all. Were you in the war, sir? That is, the first war?"

"Yes, but I didn't see much fighting," he said, closing the photo album and setting it down on the coffee table before he spoke again. He never did look directly at me while he spoke, but kept his eyes on the album, and I got the feeling he was really talking to his son instead of me.

"I was only sixteen when I enlisted because they weren't that strict about age during the first war. We were all gung ho, wanting to run over there and finish it off, then come home in a few weeks, as if we were going away for the greatest vacation in our lives. A lot of my unit had never even left New York City before, let alone gone to a foreign country.

"But most of our parents were from Central Europe, you know—Italy, Hungary, Poland, even Russia—and we all hoped it would never happen again. When we got back, some of the lucky ones, we promised ourselves and our children that it would never happen again. But we, the older generation, didn't keep our promise, did we, Mark?"

"You're not to blame, sir," I said to him. "My goodness, please don't blame yourself. It couldn't be your fault."

"But we tend to take the blame nonetheless," he answered, in a shaky voice and with a tear in his eye. Then he stood up to let me know he wanted to be alone now. I understood; he needed time to sort things out in his mind. He needed the time to remember.

I left a much sadder man, but at least I'd done my duty for Jeremy. There are some things that have to be done in life, no matter how hard they are. Going to see my mother afterward was even more wonderful because I could breathe freely again, as if I'd gotten some of the grief off my chest.

The hero's welcome I received from my mother and her friends was enough to make up for the horrible trip back home. As soon as she opened the door, I thought she looked even smaller than she used to. She rushed up to me, hugging me around my waist, and her head hardly reached my collarbone. "Mamma, Mamma, it's so good to be home!"

I could see over her shoulder that there was a roomful of people waiting to meet me inside. They were just as happy as my mother was, apparently, to see Aurora's son come home with his medals on his chest.

They even asked me to speak before a group of leading citizens about the war in Europe and my Army career. I'm not much of a public speaker, but I tried to keep my speech simple, just about my own experiences, and some of the women in the audience were crying when I told them about my crew being shot down, every last one of them, except for me.

My mother's English wasn't much better than when I had left, but she didn't have to understand my words to know what I was saying. She could tell from the way the women sitting next to her took their handkerchiefs out that I was saying the right things.

Later that night, we sat in my mother's small house, which she now proudly owned, in the bright kitchen drinking coffee. She couldn't wait to hear all about Betty and Dorothy.

I took some pictures out of my wallet; they were already somewhat frayed, but it was perfectly clear to my mother that Dorothy Maria was my daughter. She looked more like me than Betty. My mother simply took the photographs and held them to her breast, whispering a prayer in Spanish and then making the sign of the cross over her face.

"So, you're back for good, my son?" she asked. I nodded. "And your new family; when are they coming?"

"As far as I know, Betty and her grandparents moved back to London to be close to the embassy, even though it makes me worried with the Germans firing their V-2s at the city. But she'll be all right, and the last news was that she and the baby will be coming over on the *Mauretania*, in February of next year. She's so tired of filling out all the paperwork and taking so many tests, Mamma, but it's all very necessary in order for her to be accepted for traveling on the ship. She's even paying her own way, Mamma, since the Army hasn't yet approved travel for the British war brides."

"It won't be easy for your wife over here, Mark, with you still in the Army Air Corps, will it?"

"I know Mamma," I said. "And I've been giving it a lot of thought. She'll be alone a lot of the time, until I'm demobilized, especially if they send me to some small town in Arizona like they say they are going to do. The Air Force doesn't have much need for gunners anymore, not in the States, so I've been thinking of signing up for the military police. I want to get some experience so that when this war is over, Mamma, I can go into law enforcement as a profession. What do you think, Mamma?"

"I think you must do what you think is best for you and your family, Mark. I know your father would be very proud of you right now. God bless him. I am proud of you, my son."

I took a long look at my mother, remembering the early days in Delta and the long hard struggle we had all endured. I was happy to hear she'd been able to save the money all us kids had sent her over the years, making it possible for her to buy the comfortable house I now sat in enjoying her company. It wasn't long before we discussed the old days and my brothers and sisters, who were scattered throughout the States, all making new lives for themselves, like me.

"How are you, Mamma?" I asked. "Are you happy living here all alone? Wouldn't you rather be in sunny California with your grandchildren?"

"I am fine here, my son. I am near your father and we talk often together. I tell him all about you, Mark, and of Carlos, who is somewhere in the Pacific. And of little Pablo, soon to be in the Army as well, like his older brothers. No, I'm not alone, my son. As you see, my life is very pleasant now, thanks to God and my children."

"Yes, I know things are better for you, Mamma, but you can't stay here alone forever! Sooner or later, you must sell this house and come to California to live near us or with us. Pappa will understand, Mamma, he will. Everything is all right now."

My mother wiped her tears. It was easier for her to cry openly now. We kissed each other good night and I went into the spare bedroom. She walked slowly into hers. *Yes*, I thought. *My father would have been proud of us all, especially my mother.*

As it turned out, he would have laughed at the irony of what eventually happened. After I picked up my wife and child at the airport, we drove straight to a little apartment outside Douglas Army Airfield, Arizona, where I was assigned to the border patrol.

Aside from doing a little undercover work, it was my job to help pick up deserters trying to cross the border at Agua Prieta. They needed someone big and burly and fluent in Spanish, and since I fit the bill, I was only too happy to do the work.

They had the system already set up. We drove to the border in an unmarked car and then picked up a Mexican policeman, who was chosen by the Douglas Police Department. Then we would drive right to the Agua Prieta red-light district, where most of the deserters stayed.

Grabbing the deserters was the easy part. Setting up was often difficult; we had to circulate in the bars and restaurants south of the border, asking a lot of questions without appearing to sound like border patrolmen. We also had to make sure the guy we were setting up was really a deserter; not everyone who spent the night in Agua Prieta was absent without leave.

When we determined which houses the deserters were staying in, I usually went around to the back of the house and stood waiting in front of the rear door. The Mexican policeman and my partner went to the front of the house, knocking on the front door and asking, "Soldados Americanos?" This was usually a signal for the GI to grab his clothes and attempt his getaway through the back door, where he would fall right into my arms.

In May 1945, the war was over in Europe. The order came down from the War Department to begin demobilizing the armed services. They had a point system based on years of service, and I was at the top of the list. I was sent to Camp Beale in California to be processed out of the Army Air Corps.

Wearing civilian clothes for the first time in years, I arrived home early in the morning while Betty was still sleeping. I tiptoed into the bedroom and embraced her before she had even opened her eyes. When she awoke and focused her eyes, she said, "But you're not Steven! You're, oh yes, I do remember your name. You're that crazy Basque husband of mine, aren't you? See? I told you I'd remember!"

"Well, it's a good thing too," I said, "since I'm about to take you and my beautiful daughter to California with me. Would you like to go there, Betty?"

"Would I? You bet I would! Have you decided where we will live and what kind of job you will take, dear?" She looked right at me, waiting for an answer.

"It's all arranged, honey. We'll live in Berkeley near the university. My application at the Associated Oil Company in Martinez has already been accepted. Is that all right with you, honey?"

Betty hugged me tightly, saying, "Wherever you go, darling, we will go too. As long as we are always together, that's all that matters."

Standing around in the motor lab, testing various types of oils and lubricants and keeping a log about oil was not for me, especially after the excitement of living through the Second World War, so I went to work for the Chrysler Corporation in San Leandro, California.

Assigned to unload boxcars on the dock, I quickly realized that I was going nowhere fast. I enrolled in some night classes in a police academy in Oakland that were sponsored by the GI Bill. In the back of my mind, I still wanted to become a law enforcement officer.

On the last night of my classes, after we had taken the finals, our instructor told us that the California Department of Corrections was looking for men who would be interested in working at San Quentin Prison in Marin County.

I wasn't crazy about the idea of working in a prison in 1948, and Betty thought that it would make me hard-hearted, having to keep the peace in such an enormous correctional institution. When I successfully passed the civil service test, I was so pleased that I took the job, hoping for the best and trying to convince Betty that I knew how to take care of myself.

"I'm not worried about that at all," she said. "What worries me is that you might grow to like the job!"

I didn't even know what was expected of me, at first, although on my first day, I was issued a solid mahogany club and then was told to take my position in the yard. On my way, I asked one of the other officers what we were supposed to do.

"You got me," he said. "I'm new here too."

Another officer told us, "Just stay loose and stand around. Pretend that you know all about it. I've been here a week and I'm just beginning to get the hang of it. One more thing that's very important: don't ever allow the cons to bunch up together. That's how the killings take place. When you tell them what to do, make sure the gunman is standing right above you on the gun walk, keeping an eye on you at all times. He is there to protect you, not the cons."

Then we parted, going to different corners of the yard. I stood by the entrance. When I looked up, sure enough, the gunman was standing directly over me. He waved, and I waved back. We were like two old friends, meeting each other purely by accident on a street corner on a sunny day, both of us free as the wind.

They didn't want anything to happen purely by accident in San Quentin. I had to be prepared for anything at all times, without looking suspicious. It was quite a job of acting, strutting around without trying to appear superior to the cons, since I wanted them to think I was just as tough as they were without appearing to be a direct threat.

Otherwise, a person could make a lot of enemies quickly, and I didn't want any enemies in San Quentin.

Remembering that the guard with the double-barreled sawed-off shotgun was standing right over me, I began to feel a bit more secure. He had the gun cradled in his arms with a strap around his neck to prevent it from accidently falling into the yard. But even a mean-looking shotgun couldn't stop the men from trying to kill one another with knives or forks or even their bare hands. In less than an hour, my first real lesson took place.

I noticed something fishy going on at one end of the yard where a large group of men had gathered. It was certainly a fight, and when I looked up at the armed guard, he gave me an okay sign with his hand, and we both took off in the direction of the fight. I started blowing my whistle and yelling at the observers to stand back. As I approached the crowd, I saw two more officers with clubs in their hands, without realizing where they had come from.

The fight was between a white and a Black inmate. I noticed that the first officer was a sergeant. I then caught a glimpse of the knife in the Black man's hand. He was stabbing the white man everywhere he could, and even after the other two officers moved in, swinging their clubs, the Black inmate kept poking the other man. I could hear a dull, sluggish sound, as if someone were hitting a pumpkin, but still the cutting went on; he wouldn't stop even though he was being clubbed.

There was blood everywhere; blood from the Black con's head and blood from the white con's body. Finally, the officers brought the Black man down and out. The white con went down by himself.

I saw the other new officer start to vomit, as the rest of us tried to get the other cons out of the yard and locked up again. As we gathered, there were rumors on everyone's lips of a race riot, and the captain told us to keep everyone inside until they cooled off.

A week later, as I was being issued my club before going on duty to relieve the first watch, an emergency call came from the mess hall:

"Officers need help. Race riot in the mess hall." We all had known that it was coming, but here it was, only a week after I'd started working.

We were cautioned to watch out for flying steel trays and then sent to the mess hall, which was divided into three sections. The whites were seated on each side, with the Blacks in the middle. Since it was break-fast time, there was mush all over the floor. Until now, they'd only been throwing things at each other and hadn't started fighting yet.

As soon as I walked across the mess hall, I began sliding across the floor, clear to the other side. I held on to a table and I got up, fighting mad, with the damned mush all over my nice clean uniform and shoes. I started swinging my club right and left, hitting everyone in my path. When the other officers saw me, they began to follow suit, which only made the riot more intense. The captain was aware that no matter what we did, it wouldn't slow down the race riot; nothing would stop it now.

The captain motioned for us to get up against the wall. I had no idea what was coming next, and I watched him go to the telephone, speak into it quickly, and then tell the sergeant to instruct the officers to take cover as soon as the gunman arrived. The sergeant asked, "Who are you talking about?" and the captain said only one word. *Pain.*

I found out later that Pain was the state executioner, a man who had no qualms at all about killing a man. As soon as the word got around that Pain was coming, the fighting stopped just as if the men had run into a stone wall.

The man stepped out onto the catwalk from the kitchen and stood looking down at us for a second; he then pumped a round of ammo into the chamber of his rifle. Never having seen this kind of action before, the new men, including me, stood and watched him as he aimed his rifle down at the cons. We thought he was bluffing, of course, since no one in his right mind would simply start shooting into a room of fifteen hundred unarmed men. At least, that's what the inexperienced among us believed. We quickly found out we were wrong.

When he let the first round go, we could hear it echoing all over the mess hall, and then I knew Pain was not bluffing. Everybody, including all the officers, made a dive for the tables, mush on the floor notwithstanding. Then Pain fired two more rounds, and I could hear the bullets ricocheting along the walls. For a moment, I felt as if I were in war-torn Europe again.

When the shooting finally stopped, the captain yelled out, "Open the door." In that instant, everyone in the room tried to squeeze through that one main door. We got the cons out from under the tables and moved together like a giant wave. At one moment, I found myself standing in the center of the doorway, and the next moment, I was outside in the yard; they had carried me along with them, and my feet never even touched the ground during the whole way out.

These riots went on for about a week, but after my initiation, I got wise and always chose a safe place to stand, never getting in anyone's way. The prison administration transferred the troublemakers to other prisons, and the ringleaders were sent to Folsom Prison.

For the next three years, I saw things happen that no one on the outside would ever have believed. I had to swallow a lot of experiences, without even being able to tell Betty about them, because she would have begged me to give up my job and do something else, anything else. I kept the job, though, taking on the permanent position of the first watch—the hours when everything seemed to happen.

We were living in Richmond, in Contra Costa County, on the other side of the bay. Each night, I would catch the ferry with two other officers who lived near me, going to the prison every night just before midnight.

On certain days of the month, especially when there was a full moon, as the ferry approached the prison, we could hear the cons yelling and raising hell, and then we'd know that we would have a rough night ahead of us.

*A rough night.* Those three words hardly do justice to the madness that we would have to watch. It seemed sometimes that we were in Bedlam, and that the lunatics were running around, baying at the moon, and doing their dances around the campfire.

The third-watch officers were always so glad to see us coming; they couldn't get out fast enough. So we would pick up where they had left off, and believe me, we'd give the state its money's worth for having hired us.

# CHAPTER TEN

MEN IN PRISON are like men anywhere else; they work, they play, they fall in love. They get jealous of one another, and then they start acting out what other men only dream of doing.

That's where the great difference lies; men in prison step over the line of the strict codes of moral behavior that men on the outside would never breach.

Men in prison love one another and kill one another and become husband and wife. Men in prison seldom live normal lives after they have served their sentences because the lives they had in prison seemed to rob them of their humanity, of their sense of right and wrong, or at least of the limits that most men would never dare to cross.

I didn't see enough of my family during the years I was working at San Quentin, and I hardly ever ate at home since I frequently lost my appetite after seeing men maul one another like tigers and then kiss and make up like doves.

In the beginning of my life as a prison guard I used to tell Betty about the cons and almost everything about my duties there, but now Betty was pregnant with our second child and I purposely avoided any discussion about my life and the prison.

I remember the first talk the warden had with me. It was the kind of pep talk I might have expected from a pro football coach before the team went out on the field but with a deadly undercurrent that made me more aware of the warden's position regarding me and the cons.

"The number one thing to remember, Vergara, is there are plenty of homemade Saturday night specials here, and even though they may look like a pipe with a block of wood roped around the end, they're still lethal, believe me!" He looked right at me before continuing his pep talk, and I assure you, he had my undivided attention.

"If you should ever be taken hostage, held at knifepoint or gunpoint, if you should be taken by an inmate and held hostage, and if the ransom is to open the gate and let the inmate free, our rule is this: we never open the gate, never for anyone, and that includes you and me!

"The most important thing I can tell you is to stay on your toes and expect the worst at all times. Never get conned by the inmates who are being nice to you or being polite or offering you some kind of gift. Never take a gift from a con, and never let him get too friendly, understand? There are only two kinds of people at San Quentin: the good guys and the bad guys, and the bad guys at this prison are really bad, Vergara."

Not all the inmates were killers, and I learned to trust some more than others. The warden even thought he could train some of them to learn a trade or finish high school. He called it rehabilitation, something fairly new in the penal system at that time.

He cared about them; we all did. Sometimes it took more patience than I ever knew I possessed. We weren't supposed to lose our tempers. We were not meant to see certain acts the inmates did, even though we would hear them, but we couldn't tell anyone about what we saw. Sometimes I felt like one of those monkeys that see no evil, hear no evil, speak no evil.

Another time the warden told us, "If an inmate even so much as strikes an officer, then he will remain in prison for the rest of his life. If an inmate ever draws blood or disables you, he'll be automatically executed."

That was California law in 1949, and I felt somewhat easier after I heard him say that because I knew that the cons knew it too, and they would have to be insane to try to hurt a guard. But cons are only human, and we could never tell for sure how sane they were. Some would explode for no reason or go on a rampage, sometimes taking one of us with them.

By the time our second child, Mark Jr., was born, I had already witnessed enough violence and sadism at San Quentin to make me wonder how sane it was to bring children into this world. Nothing could have stopped me from wanting to have children with Betty, but after one particular incident at the prison, I began to wish that I'd chosen another profession.

It was my first personal taste of violence, and I was almost ashamed of myself for having lost control over my emotions. A man can take only so much violence without giving some back, and I lost my temper on a few occasions, although I didn't always regret it afterward.

I was assigned to B section of the East Block, where some of the cons were segregated from the rest. They were held separately for a variety of reasons: some refused to work or had disobeyed orders; others had venereal diseases and were quarantined to prevent the spreading of their illness. There were also the finks who needed the extra protection of being kept away from the other convicts. One fink never left his area for a whole year; when he finally went into the yard, he lasted only a day. They found him in what we called *Rape Alley*, with his throat slashed and his tongue cut out. That's what they did to informers in San Quentin.

Rape Alley was a story in itself, but the words are clear enough to describe what happened there, mostly to the newer, younger men. If they happened to be good-looking, then one of the older cons would claim them, turning them into queens. Sooner or later, it happened to almost everyone who wasn't already a swordsman, the male, or a jocker, the innocent new guy in the cell block.

Strangely enough, I accepted the fact that these cons fell in love with each other, since being physically isolated from women narrowed down the choices for any sexual contact. The new men usually fought it at first. I remember a kid named Ronnie who had been sent up from Lancaster, an institution for wayward boys and juvenile delinquents.

Ronnie put up a valiant struggle in the beginning. He had become so uncontrollable in Lancaster that he'd been transferred to the joint, and he came in spitting fire, really putting on an act, as if he were the toughest guy who'd ever darkened the doors of a prison.

Ronnie was so proud that he'd made it to the big time that he openly strutted around, having no idea of what he was letting himself in for when he met Big George.

Big George was in for manslaughter and arson, among many other things. First, he found out which cell Ronnie had been put into. Then he sent out inquiries to see if Ronnie had any money or anything valuable to use as barter. Then he started to send the kid presents, such as cigarettes, candy, aftershave lotion, and other things that he might like to have.

"Where did these things come from?" Ronnie wanted to know, and everyone told him they came from Big George. That was all he needed to know. Even if Ronnie hid these presents under his bunk at first, he'd get around to using them sooner or later. And that's when Big George cashed in on his investment. He bided his time, watching Ronnie carefully in the yard and finding ways to sit next to him in the mess hall, and then he said, nonchalantly, "Did you like that box of candy, kid?"

"Sure," Ronnie said. "So what?"

"So, maybe you'd like more candy sometime, huh, kid? Candy or some other sweet things? All you have to do is say yes, and I'll make arrangements with your cell partner to exchange places with him for tonight."

Ronnie didn't say yes right away, and when Big George didn't score, it made him so angry that he arranged to have the kid taken care of down in rape alley. There weren't enough officers to protect everybody and prevent the rapes and beatings that went on. Sometimes, if the kid put up a fight, the jockers would cut him up or even kill him. These men had made their lives into a hell, and killing another man meant nothing to them. Homosexuality was responsible for at least 80 percent of the killings at San Quentin, and this figure would probably be the same in other maximum-security prisons as well.

After Ronnie was raped several times, he started getting little presents again from Big George, who had a lot of time on his hands and all the patience in the world. Sooner or later the new kid would have to give in and say yes, since it was his only alternative.

As soon as Ronnie agreed to become Big George's wife, the word went out that everyone else should keep their hands off. Sometimes the queens weren't allowed to talk to anyone else. The worst thing that could happen to a queen was to be caught in the act of coitus with another man. In the prison system of morality, this meant an automatic divorce, and we would put the queen into the segregated Queens' Row, and then the jocker might as well start looking for another kid to reform.

The prison's policy, once a queen, always a queen, meant that someone like Ronnie would live out the rest of her sentence on Queens' Row until she was finally released, and I use the word *she* because we thought of all the queens as being female. Some of the cons grew to like their roles as females, parading around to get the attention of the cons working anywhere near them.

We had a lot of trouble with poisonings. At first, we couldn't figure out how and where the queens were getting the poison, but then we noticed they were very adept at keeping their flower garden neat, especially their geranium patch.

One day an officer noticed some of the queens picking geraniums and rubbing the flowers on their lips and cheeks to substitute for makeup. A little while later, one of them became very sick and was taken to the hospital, where it was found that she had indeed been poisoned. At that point, all the geraniums were removed from the queens' compound, which was the original cell block in the prison.

This compound had solid steel doors with one six-by-six-inch peephole. The walls were so thick that if a queen became sick or decided to slit her throat and then yell for help, no one would have ever heard her. For that reason, we made frequent checks with our flashlights to see that everything was all right inside. There were no toilet facilities there; each queen had her own bucket, which was emptied out in the morning at lineup time. After being inside all night with their honey buckets, there was often a good fight in the morning. The tension would build up during the night to such a pitch that we never knew what to expect when the queens woke up. As often as not, when these catfights would get started, the officer up on the gun rail would have to fire some warning shots into the air to break up the fights and settle everyone back to earth again.

The queens adopted female names and the officers referred to them by their chosen names. Only when we submitted an official report was their real name ever mentioned. One of the queens, Lillian, was arrested by the LAPD, legally charged, and turned over to the LA County sheriff for detention. When she went before the judge, she was convicted to the Tehachapi women's prison. Being somewhat of a joker, she went along with her conviction, never saying a word about her true identity.

The truth came out when she was being admitted and was forced to take her clothes off for a shower. Lillian protested that she wasn't feeling well and didn't want to take a shower because she had her period. The female correctional officer assigned to her insisted that the sanitary napkin be removed or it would come off the hard way. Reluctantly, Lillian started to take off her undergarments, and finally, everything was forcibly removed. She was immediately transferred to San Quentin.

Maybe if she had stayed at Tehachapi, she would have given up pretending to be a woman, with all those women around her. In any case, Lillian was the only bit of comic relief we had at the joint for a long time, so we told the story often to any of the new officers or inmates who would listen.

Betty didn't think it was all that amusing. She was beginning not to even ask me what kind of a night I'd had, after I got home from work. She knew that I worked the death watch from time to time, and on those mornings, after witnessing an execution, I'd come home and go straight into the bedroom, not even answering her if she called out my name.

It's one thing to see a plane blown out of the air by an enemy bomber; it's even bearable to watch one man kill another in a fight because you always hope that until the very last minute, one of the combatants will pull away or stop or that someone else will interfere and put an end to it all.

But it takes a very strong stomach to sit quietly by as a man is strapped into a chair in a large, glass-walled chamber, then locked in to wait for the cyanide capsule to drop, and then to wait for the man to take his last breath. The warden used to tell these men to take a really deep beath, since it would knock them out and they would suffer less.

"When I give you the signal," he would explain, "then breathe deeply and you won't feel a thing after that if the gas is present."

These executions were supposed to start at ten o'clock in the morning precisely. But sometimes the gas capsule wouldn't drop, and the prisoner would take a big breath, inhaling deeply, and nothing would happen. He'd look at the warden and shake his head, as if to say that the gas hadn't reached him yet. After it finally hit him, the man would start to struggle for air, then slump forward with his head on his chest. By ten fifteen, the struggle would be over, his face muscles would relax, and the fluid from his eyes, nose, and mouth would start to ooze out, dropping onto his lap.

At exactly ten thirty, his head would begin to lift up and he would finally come to rest with his head facing the ceiling. The doctor would pronounce him dead, and then everyone would leave. At eleven o'clock, the blower would be turned on and all the gas would be blown out of the chamber.

It was my job to keep the peace in the audience watching the execution. There were often newspaper reporters and preachers, and on some rare occasions, relatives of the victims were allowed to witness the execution. Often the clergymen would get carried away, praying out loud and disturbing the other witnesses, so I would have to escort them outside.

Many of the prisoners preferred to stay with the warden instead of a priest during their last night. He gave them as much comfort as possible and sometimes sent an officer all the way into San Francisco for some special ingredients for the prisoner's last meal.

Even though she never said this in so many words, I think Betty was disappointed that I took my job so seriously. My eyes had been wide open when I signed the contract to work there. We had been married only five years, but she knew me well enough by then to know that a Basque does what he has to without complaining or asking anyone else to do the work for him, and without changing his mind.

She never asked me whether I liked the work. Maybe if she had asked me whether I really enjoyed being a correctional officer, I might have realized even more quickly that the job wasn't really for me. I hated to admit that perhaps I had made a mistake, so I stuck it out as long as I could, until one terrible day when the violence began to affect me so strongly that I hit a con so hard he was unconscious for a week.

One night, while assigned to the goon squad, I was called in to help another guard. I was told that one of the cons had had a breakdown and was raising hell, keeping the other cons awake and stirring them up. When a con was put into isolation for twenty-six days, with nothing but a cement slab, cement pillow, and one blanket in his cell, we started looking for him to break on the thirteenth day. Very few made it all the way to the full twenty-six days.

We went over to his cell and opened the peephole. As we did, we both jumped back in shock. The man's face was right up against the opening. His eyes were as wide as saucers and we could tell that he was just staring blankly, without even seeing us. We told the con to step back, which he finally did reluctantly.

*This man has really flipped his cork*, I thought. He just kept mumbling to come and get him. After we opened the steel door, we told him that we were going to take him out of isolation, but he wasn't listening. I knew he didn't hear us. The sergeant said we would have to take him out the hard way.

"Okay," I said in a low voice, even though the con didn't understand my words. "I'll get behind him and try to hold him. Then you guys grab his arms and lead him out of the cell."

I faked him out by pretending that I was going to poke out his eyes, which gave me an advantage because while he blinked, I got behind him and began to push. But now the sergeant and the new officer just stood there. "Come on, gimme a hand," I shouted, but the con was too much for us, grabbing the only club from the new officer's hand and bringing it over his shoulder. Every time he took a swing, he hit me with the club, over and over again, even though I tried as hard as I could to dodge the blows. Every other swing seemed to land on either my arms or my back and shoulders.

Finally, I yelled out, "Get the goddamn club from him. Don't just stand there!"

The new man seemed hesitant to approach, but the sergeant pushed him and together they finally got the club away from the con and threw him back up against the wall; then they ran toward the door, where other officers were standing. I picked up the club, and the con and I charged at each other, our heads down, coming at each other like two bulls. I raised the club, and as he looked up for a second, I brought it down and caught him right above his forehead. The blow echoed through the cell block. Two streams of blood spurted from his head, and he was out cold.

The man had done nothing serious to me, and yet I had come pretty close to killing him. They took him to the infirmary, and I never saw him again after that.

I had broken another man's arm once and met him years later on the street. He came up to me and said, "Don't I know you from somewhere?"

The thought I had at that moment was that he remembered me from prison and would probably want to kill me now.

He said, "It's Vergara, isn't it? How could I ever forget you? You came swinging at me one day, in the joint, and I ended up in the hospital with my arm in a cast for months! But you know, all that time I spent in the hospital gave me a chance to think about my life for the first time. All those months I walked around with my arm mending, I decided that I'd go straight from then on. I've got a job now, and I'm married, with a baby at home. I made it, Vergara! I guess I've always wanted to thank you for helping me straighten out. You did it, I think. I guess sometimes you have to break before you can heal up again."

I was pleased that my own anger had changed this man's life, but when he said that bit about having to break before he could become healed, I remembered what we meant in the joint when we said that a con had broken.

These episodes of my time at San Quentin affected me so deeply that I guess it was the straw that broke the camel's back. After these incidents, I decided to give up my job and move on. The warden had told me that there are only good guys and bad guys in prison, and I wasn't feeling so much like a good guy after my anger got the better of me. I had seen good executions, men walking bravely with smiles on their faces, waving good-bye to life as if it were all a big joke, and bad executions, prisoners who had killed in cold blood, one his entire family, screaming and crying out as he was being led into the execution chamber that it wasn't fair to take him because there were so many other prisoners on death row who had been there so much longer than he had. It made me sick to see this man crying out for his own life when he had taken the lives of his wife and children.

After witnessing the terrible slaughter of three officers by a con who had hidden himself in the library and killed every man who walked into his ambush, I knew it was time for me to give up my promise that I could handle anything. The place had hardened my heart, and it wouldn't have been fair to Betty or the children for me to keep working in that madhouse.

I wrote the warden my letter of resignation, and on my last ferry trip back home, I didn't even turn around.

I had stayed in the Air Force Reserves, and as it happened, my branch of service was recalling all reserve units back to active duty because of the Korean conflict. I couldn't get back fast enough.

# CHAPTER ELEVEN

I WAS ONLY in my middle thirties, but I had aged a decade at San Quentin, and my hair was already turning gray. I had been spending so much time at work and worrying about it even when I went home in the mornings that I had grown apart from my own family. Now was the time I would catch up with them, for they seemed to be running ahead of me, without waiting for their old man to get in step with them.

Everything would be different now. I was back on active duty with the Air Force. I would finally take part in the family, sitting where I belonged at the head of the table and helping to keep peace at home without ever again thinking of convicts or criminals, killers or rapists.

That was my dream, at any rate, and when I found out that I'd be stationed at March Air Force Base, in Riverside, California, I picked myself up to get ready for the move.

The Air Force had changed a great deal from my day; it had even broken off from the Army in 1947 and was adjusting to self-rule. I was almost like a new recruit enjoying my new lifestyle and feeling a part of the civilized world again.

I was assigned an Air Police flight that consisted of ten men who maintained law and order within the compounds of the base. As operations sergeant, I was ultimately in charge of all law enforcement activities, and one of my responsibilities was to rewrite the Standard Operating Procedures Manual for all law enforcement personnel.

In the latter part of 1952, the bomber wing was sent on temporary duty to Upper Heyford in England for ninety days. I was to accompany the wing with four hundred other men. Betty was fuming that she could not come along with me, and she made me promise to visit her grandparents.

After promising a hundred times and kissing my family of five now—with little baby Jeremy—good-bye for three months, I set off with the others to help organize the flight-line security field at Upper Heyford. My dream of family life hadn't lasted too long. This was to be the first of many separations in my new career.

I had never been prepared for tragedy to strike. I'd seen crippled B-17 bombers crash before, exploding on ground contact because their landing gear had failed. I'd seen terrible accidents caused by a rock or a bit of cement sparking the 100 percent octane fuel to ignite. But we were in peacetime now in England. When one of our C-47s returning from North Africa crashed on our base, it threw bodies outside of its belly like a giant whale exploding and pouring its guts out, including parts of the plane itself, landing three or four blocks from the point of impact.

The smell was unbearable, lingering around the crash site for days. Seeing the broken and burning bodies made me aware again of my own mortality, reminding me of the fragile thread that connects us to life and to our loved ones.

My first three-day pass was to be spent visiting Betty's grandparents in London. I had written to let them know I was coming, and I knew they'd be very surprised to see me after so many years, but I wasn't prepared for the great kindness they showed me, treating me like a long-lost son.

As soon as they led me into their sitting room, I saw framed pictures of Betty and the children everywhere. On the mantelpiece and all across the piano top, there were pictures of the children, ranging in age from three or four months to eight years. I had realized that

Betty had been sending pictures all these years, but now, to see my own family in a gallery of Vergara photographs made my heart burst with paternal pride and happiness.

After we sat down to tea, Pop asked me right away, "So, what have you been doing all these years?"

"Do you mean that Betty hasn't written you all about it?" I leaned back and started to laugh. "I would have thought you'd know every detail by now, Pop."

"Not exactly," Nan said, offering me a plate of scones. "We know when Dorothy cut her first tooth and how many pounds Mark Jr. weighed at birth and all of Jeremy's physical attributes, including moles and birthmarks, but we've hardly heard anything about you, Mark dear. As a matter of fact you're quite the mystery man around here."

I drank my tea and thought for a good long minute before I spoke. "Maybe Betty hasn't told you much about me because I haven't been around her for a long time. I mean that my work has taken me away from my family, and I still have that Basque quality of wanting to spend my time with other men, like me.

"You know, there's a part of the country, in the state of Utah, where practically all the sheepherders are Basque. Maybe you don't know much about them, but they are a solitary breed. Their work always comes first, and because of it, they are often away from their wives and families for months at a time.

"I must take after my father, Nan. He enjoyed being in the company of men. He was raised around all kinds of stock and became an expert in the handling of cattle. Did I ever tell you that as a young man my father was a bullfighter? His quadrille traveled throughout the Latin American countries and Spain, several times. To this day, his name appears in the Bullfighting Museum in Barcelona, Spain. There is also an avenue named after him, did you know that? It is the avenue leading to the University of Medicine in Madrid.

"Someday, I will take Betty and the children to the Basque Country, my father's homeland. I've always wanted to go there, ever since I was a child."

I paused for a moment, thinking of what Nan had said. "I never intentionally kept my working life a secret from Betty, but there were just some things about prison life that I couldn't have told her. So I guess I wanted to protect her from the cruelty and inhumanity of it all."

They respected my silence then, and no one spoke until Pop cleared his throat and told me, "That's how we brought her up, you know, trying to shield her from the horrors of the war. Her mother, Dorothy, our only daughter, was killed in the first year of the war. If it hadn't been for Betty, I don't know what we would have done or how we would have got through it, Mark."

"Do you mean that Betty helped you in some way?" I asked.

"Helped us?" Nan quickly replied. "Oh my Lord, yes! And if you think it was the other way around, you're mistaken, my dear. Of course, we clothed her and fed her, but she was the one who made it all worthwhile after her mother died. You can't possibly know what it's like to lose a child of your own, and I hope to God you will never find out, Mark."

I sat looking at them both as they were deep in thought with their own memories, and I couldn't help but remember my own mother when my little sister had died. But I said nothing, for I knew that Nan had more she wanted to say.

"Betty was such a good little girl. She was a single child, just like her mother, so she was used to playing alone or being in the company of grown-ups. She read a great deal and was extremely clever, but I think she was terribly lonely without her mother. We were lonely too. Oh yes, Bert, don't shake your head that way and try to deny it, my dear."

She turned to her husband, who had put his cup down and was shaking his head.

"No, don't misunderstand me, sweetheart," he said. "I was only thinking how we were blessed, in a way, by having the chance to live through Dorothy's childhood twice. I don't mean that Betty and her mother were exactly the same, but if Betty hadn't lived with us all those good years, then Dorothy would have faded away in our memories like a dream. Every time I looked at little Betty, I remembered her mother. It was only natural, you understand, but it helped me go on living. Isn't that right, Nan?"

She had bowed her head and was crying softly. Then she fumbled in her lap, looking for a napkin or a handkerchief to dry her eyes with. As she sniffled, her face brightened up and she said, "Aren't we lucky, though, to have our little Betty's husband here with us now? I do wish I could meet my great-grandchildren, though. It's the only sorrow in my life."

"And I wish you could meet them too," I told her. "I wish that I could take you both back with me when my tour of duty expires here in England. Maybe next year Betty and the children can come back to see you both for a month. I'll do my best to make that happen for them, and for you both, I promise."

"Well, at least we can take your picture, to prove you've actually been here!" Pop said, getting up to find his old Brownie camera, bought from a GI on a street corner in London almost a decade before.

We posed for pictures, first me and Nan together, with Pop acting as photographer and then me and Pop together, with Nan acting as photographer, then Nan with me. It was the most fun I'd had in a long time, and we kept laughing so hard that when Betty and I finally received the copies, she asked me why I was crying.

"Crying?" I replied, and I could tell why she had thought so; my face looked contorted, showing an expression somewhere between pleasure and pain. It was really only openmouthed laughter that made me look so funny, the laughter that comes from the heart and can only come when you're with the best of friends or with the people you really love.

On our way home from temporary duty, we stopped in the Azores, and since I was the only man who could speak even a smattering of Portuguese, I was the official interpreter for the evening. Even as my buddies and I were having dinner together, toasting one another and comparing notes on the late Christmas presents we were bringing home to our families, I kept thinking of my in-laws, knowing, for some strange reason, that I would never see them again. Pop died the following year. He was eighty-seven years old.

It must have been terribly hard for Nan, who had lived with her husband for more than fifty years. But she took it bravely, like the strong and courageous women in my own family who had suffered terrible misfortunes. She took it truly like a Basque. And if anyone ever asks me what qualities a Basque woman has, I tell them, just as I told Betty's friend Marky when she came to console Betty.

"Marky," I said, "regardless of her years, she is a tough and very proud lady. One who walks with her head held high and always has a wide smile on her face and a gentle touch for those around her.

"You would immediately recognize a Basque woman by her strength and courage and her great sense of determination and loyalty to her family. Even her hearty meals are prepared with great pride and joy, the same pride and joy she exudes at a Basque festival, watching her handsome husband and sons compete in a woodchopping contest or sweep a wicker chistera and slam the dog-hide ball against the wall of a fronton. Yes, Marky, a Basque woman is unique, just as Betty's nan is."

It took Betty a long time to get over the shock of losing her beloved grandfather, especially not being able to be with her grandmother when she felt she was needed most. We made a promise to ourselves that we would save up enough money for her and the children to travel back to England the following year, and we each lived with those thoughts as we worked harder and harder to achieve that goal.

I was beginning to feel really good about myself; everything was going well in my life. I was proud of my accomplishments, happy with my family, and even getting over the nightmares that I still had from time to time, all revolving around my years at San Quentin. Well, I should have known better than to take such happiness for granted because life had always thrown me for a loop whenever I least expected it. I should have been suspicious of my newfound peace of mind, and I should have realized from my past experience that when any one of my three children got sick, the others would get the disease too, sooner or later. But I never expected them all to come down with scarlet fever at the same time.

As soon as I heard the words *scarlet fever*, I thought of my mother, who had almost died of it. Words have the power to frighten us, to inspire devotion, even to move us to tears. The words *scarlet fever* had always brought out the fear of death in my heart and soul, and my knees grew weak when I heard that all my children had the dreaded disease.

I'd been coming home from the flight line early in the morning, just in time to watch Betty get the children ready for school. I'd sit and watch her brushing Dorothy's hair, putting little ribbons on each side. Then they'd dress the boys, who always looked so clean and cute. After a final mad rush to finish dressing herself, Betty would drop the boys off at preschool, deliver Dorothy to the front steps of the grammar school, and finally make it to her own job, just in the nick of time.

This was the American dream; I thought we had everything—a family, nice home, good jobs, even a mongrel puppy picked up on the street corner, and most of all, a feeling of security about the future.

But it never occurred to me that I had been sleepwalking in that dream. I guess I'd never taken enough time to speculate about my role in the family. After all, I'd come home to a hot meal waiting for me.

All I had to do was take my shoes off, loosen my belt, and sit down to enjoy my family. But I never stopped for even a moment to wonder how everything kept working so smoothly and efficiently, that is, until the children got sick.

When the doctor came to see them, he kept shaking his head and making a *tsk, tsk* sound with his tongue. "This is bad," he finally said to Betty and me. "Very bad indeed."

Poor Betty almost fainted just from looking at the man. "Well, how bad is it? You can be honest with me," she told him. "What can we all do to help them survive this?"

Then the doctor broke out in a grin, his face turning serious again in the very next moment. "They'll require around-the-clock attention. You'll have to call in a relative or someone to help you, because they will need washing three times a day, a complete change of all clothing and bedding each time, and medication on time, around the clock. I don't envy you, but they can all survive, with the proper care."

Betty immediately answered, "Oh, I'll give them the proper care. You don't have to worry about that."

As the doctor was leaving, he took a good look at my wife and said, "It's not the children I'm worried about."

I didn't even understand right away what he meant by that parting remark, but it dawned on me slowly, watching Betty get up all through the night, every night, making special liquid foods and juices for the children, changing them after bathing them three or four times a day, and washing clothes continuously, while she comforted them by reading their favorite books out loud and singing songs to them and doing all the hundred things that a loving mother does with her sick children.

Every day the doctor came to check on the children, and he would say to Betty, "Is your family helping you?"

"I have no family, except for my children."

That, of course, should have tipped me off right away. I should have known that she was wearing herself beyond her own endurance. But

I didn't realize it until I came home from work one morning. I'd been doing shift work, on duty all day for one week, then every evening for a week, then every night for a week.

That morning when I got home and found Betty lying very still in bed, I went up to her and saw quite clearly that she wasn't sleeping; her eyes were large and firmly focused on the ceiling light. There was no expression on her face, just a blank look. She didn't say hello or acknowledge my presence in any way. She didn't even seem to know that I'd come into the room and was standing right next to her.

I reached down and held her, but she didn't say a word.

"Is anything wrong, honey?" I asked, shaking her gently. "What's wrong, honey?" Over and over again I asked.

Then I went into the children's room. Dawn was just breaking outside the window and Dorothy said, "Mummy had to lie down, Daddy. She didn't feel too good. Is she okay now?"

"She's fine," I replied to my precious daughter. "She is just tired, that's all. She needs a little rest too. She'll be okay after a nap. How are you doing, honey, and how are your brothers?"

"We're all feeling better now, Daddy, but I'm sure glad you're home now."

I let Dorothy go back to sleep and called the doctor right away. He came over as soon as he could and finally explained to me that Betty had suffered an exhaustion breakdown.

"She needs complete bed rest for at least ten days. Try to let her be quiet. I told her to get some help in caring for the children. I kept asking her if anyone was helping her, but she never answered me. You could put them all in the base hospital. They'd get proper care there."

The way he looked at me in that moment made my blood boil. He was absolutely right, of course. I knew he was implying that I should have been there to help my wife. He seemed to be saying (or my bad conscience was trying to let me know) that if only I'd opened my eyes and taken a good look around me, I would have seen that Betty was getting weaker and more tired with each passing day.

I immediately applied for an emergency leave, and for the next ten days, I quickly learned how it felt to be a twenty-four-hour caretaker of four sick people.

I came to acknowledge Betty's enormous role in my life, doing everything for all of us as well as keeping her own job outside the home as the secretary in a downtown office and going to school at night for her American citizenship.

I made up my mind then and there that my family would start coming first in my life. No more weekend hunting trips with the boys from the squadron, no more fishing trips to Ensenada, not unless we all went together as a family.

In time, we pulled through that emergency, and the more responsibilities I assumed, the more I enjoyed myself. I was working in Riverside on town patrol, and Betty and I were finally able to get a new three-bedroom house right on the base. There was a new school right across the street, and we even managed to buy a new car. Our first! So it was the beginning of a new phase in my life and the end of an old one. I would now be a family man, instead of just a man with a family.

The words *scarlet fever* still had the power to frighten the living daylights out of me, but my family's sickness made me truly aware of my responsibilities to them and my great love for them all.

# CHAPTER TWELVE

IT WAS EXTREMELY hot in the summer of 1952. The orange groves were filled with lush green trees bearing sweet fruit, and the sky was clear and blue. The San Bernardino Mountains were visible for miles around, and bright red bougainvillea bloomed from trellises against the white stucco houses. As I played catch with my boys in the school playground, I thanked my lucky stars, knowing that I was a truly lucky man.

This was the first morning of our annual vacation. Betty and Dorothy were preparing a picnic basket as the boys and I got the car ready for our trip to Ensenada, Mexico. We were all very excited. The children were making more noise than the fireworks on the Fourth of July. As we loaded up the car and packed ourselves inside it, I started whistling a happy tune, oblivious to the sounds of celebration drumming in my ears.

*After all*, I thought, *what better time to let off steam?* We were going on vacation as a family, and we could make as much noise as we wanted to.

After about ten minutes of it, I wished I could turn around and go back home, fall asleep in my armchair in front of the TV, or listen to a baseball game on the radio. *This is what Betty has to endure all by herself most of the time*, I thought to myself, turning to look at her in the seat next to me. I wondered how she did it without going crazy.

"Okay, let's calm down, everyone," I said, turning my voice up a few notches so they could hear in the back seat. "We're going to have a good time, but we're going to do it quietly! Do you understand, all of you?"

I heard, "Yes, Daddy," from all of them, one by one. For a second, I seemed to be reliving my own childhood, when my father would ask all of us if we understood him whenever he told us to be quiet. "Yes, Pappa, I understand," I could hear myself saying as a ten-year-old.

As I drove along the coast, nearing San Diego, my mind went back in time, remembering what it had been like for me to be the man of the family. I used to pray to God, asking him to bring a new father into my life, someone to help me carry the burden of being the oldest son. I used to even pray that my mother would find another man to marry, but, of course, she never did.

*But it was all wishful thinking*, I said to myself as my own children suddenly shouted out that they could see the mighty waves of the Pacific Ocean crashing against the craggy rocks just outside the window. We could see the uncrowded beaches, and some ships were visible on the horizon, looking like toys so far out to sea.

My mind went back to my mother, and I wondered whether I only thought I was the head of the house, whether it was my mother who did everything after Father died. Bless her soul! Did I think that I was helping her? Was I only pretending to be a man, acting as if I were older than ten years?

I shook my head and started laughing at myself, and Betty asked, "Why are you laughing, dear?"

"It's nothing," I told her. "I'm just happy, being on vacation with my family."

My character was being formed in those early years, and even though I was only ten, I did the work of a man, going to school only when the beet harvesting had been done, learning games with friends only after the other children had been fed for the night and put to bed.

*My poor dear mother*, I thought, remembering some of the things she had told me later in her life.

"I was stricken with scarlet fever and was ill for many months after your birth, my son. The midwife had to move into our house and take on all the responsibilities of caring for you. Many times, I came so very close to death, and I wasn't even able to hold you in my arms until you were almost five months old. It was during my convalescence that I had so many strange dreams, almost visions, that appeared suddenly and would not leave my tired, troubled inner self. It was as if the Angel of Death was standing or hovering over me then, face-to-face, debating whether I would live or die.

"I could hear you crying sometimes, distant cries, even though you were only in the next room. Your cries seemed to be coming through a veil or mist. I would try to reach out for you and raise myself up from the bed, knowing you needed me, but the Angel of Death held me down, Mark. I was as close to death as I had been as a child with the smallpox. But I was now a woman with three young babies to care for, and I had escaped to the New World. I wanted to hang on to life more than ever.

"I kept telling the angel to go away, but every morning as the sun came up, I would see him standing at the bedroom window as the curtains blew all around him and through him, and he would whisper to me, 'One more day, Aurora,' calling me by the name I had been given as a child. 'Yes, Rosita, you may have one more day.'

"I prayed so hard, and I thanked the Lord for every day he gave me. I promised him that I would care for you and that you would never hear a harsh word from my lips. I would try to shield you and your sisters from all the misery and suffering that existed in the world.

"When your father finally joined me in our bed, sleeping at my side as he had always done, I knew then that the Good Lord had heard my prayers. I kept my promise, Mark, for it was the easiest thing in the world for me to love you, since you were my first son.

"I kept my promise to the Lord and spent more time with you than the other children, for in my suffering, you had suffered too. I even carried you on my back like the peasants in the old country do with their infants and would often turn to kiss your little head, leaning against my shoulder.

"But I never fully kept my promise to the good Lord, Mark. Not after your father died. I always told him how very sorry I was that I had failed in my promise. Life was so very hard for us, especially you, my son. You became the head of the family. You had the responsibilities no ten-year-old should ever have to endure. You were my strength and you did so much to help me and the little ones. Yes, Mark, I thanked the good Lord every day for you, my son."

*Yes*, I thought, *life was hard for us all in those early days*. But the Vergaras were always proud and accepting of their adversities, even Sanchez and his tight knot of little stinking men at the Lincoln Rooms. I would continue to carry on the proud Basque beliefs and traditions and instill them in my own children, teaching them to work and play hard, and having a fierce pride in our background.

"You are so quiet, darling," Betty said to me. "Are you feeling all right?"

"I'm on top of the world, honey. I feel great."

"That's good. I'm loving this. Isn't the scenery beautiful, Mark?"

"Yes, California is truly God's country. Look at that Pacific Ocean—isn't it inviting? The beaches along here are just about the best in the world. How about we all go in for dip?"

"Let's wait until after we visit the mission. Besides, Dorothy and Mark Jr. are napping right now, dear."

I looked over at Betty, holding Jeremy on her lap, and remembered when my third child had been born. Jeremy was perhaps a foreign name for a grandson of a Basque. His name was a compromise between Betty's favorite, Jeffrey, and my own. We ended up both being satisfied, and after all, our sons had my last name, their grandfather's name, to give to their own sons when I would be a grandfather too.

I was a proud father and a lucky man to have Betty as my wife. I, too, thanked God for the many blessings he had bestowed upon me. I, too, made a promise to him, that I would never let my children suffer the miseries of life as I had as a child. But I had Betty to help me.

It's no wonder I let Betty take over the care of our own family. I was beginning to understand that I'd never had much of a childhood myself after my father died. I guess I was trying to make up for it by being away from Betty and the children so much of the time, enjoying myself with my buddies, knowing my own family was being well cared for.

We stopped to visit San Diego de Alcalá, the first mission built in San Diego, by Friar Junipero Serra, and as we wandered through the beautiful old building, kneeling to pray for a few minutes in the cool, peaceful chapel, I remembered something that my crewmate Jeremy had said to me during one of our long conversations as we lay in our bunks, talking in low voices all through the night.

He seemed much wiser about some things than I was, and he seemed much older when he said, "Maybe you joined the Army to find him."

"To find who?" I asked. "Or should I say, to find whom?"

"Well, you were just telling me that you felt lost when your father died. So maybe you thought you could find a substitute, someone to take his place in the Army."

"I joined the Army," I said defensively, "because my country is at war. And anyway, how do you know so much about all of this psychology business?"

"Don't change the subject, Mark," he said, trying to laugh off my remarks. "I'm planning to be a good psychologist when this is all over, and I've just been reading *Civilization and Its Discontents*, by Sigmund Freud, so I know all about man's need to find a god outside of himself and worship him."

"Now, wait a minute. Wait a doggone minute," I replied, sitting up on the edge of my bed and leaning over so I wouldn't have to shout. "Finding a father substitute and worshipping God are two different things altogether. You don't seem to realize that I'm talking about a ten-year-old who needed someone in the flesh to help him take care of his family! At ten years old, I wasn't looking for God! I was looking for a man, just a man, to help me make some day-to-day decisions about my brothers and sisters. I wasn't looking for God, Jeremy!"

"Now, don't get all worked up about this, Mark," he said, "or I'll end up thinking that you're protesting too much, which only means that you're denying the truth because you can't accept it."

"I give up!" I told him. "I can never win, having a discussion with you!"

"This isn't a competition, you know," Jeremy quipped. "I don't want to win this discussion. I'm just telling you what I think about your own life. It's true for all men, you know, not just you, Mark. All of us need a father figure to emulate, to use as a model. If we don't have a father's love while we're growing up, if we're never encouraged and praised and made to feel that we're worthy of love, then we're bound to keep searching for it when we are adults. So, I'm only suggesting that you chose the Army as a substitute to fulfill that need."

"Now I know you're nuts, Jeremy!" I said, lying back down in my bunk with my hands crossed under my head as a kind of pillow. I knew I wouldn't be able to sleep for a long time. I couldn't get his words out of my mind.

My youngest son, Jeremy, was pulling on my sleeve. "Let's go, Daddy," he said. When I looked up, I saw that Betty, Dorothy, and Mark Jr. had already left the chapel and were waiting outside in the sunlight.

"All right," I told Jeremy, picking him up and carrying him out of the mission in my arms.

"Put me down, please." When I did, he ran to join the others.

"He's too old to pick up that way," Betty said to me, taking my arm as we watched the children run on ahead of us.

"How did he get too old for me to carry him?" I asked. "How did he get too old, all of a sudden?"

"It didn't happen all of a sudden, dear," Betty said. "It's been happening slowly, for the past year or so. You just haven't noticed!"

So my children had been growing up right under my nose, and my youngest was now too old to be picked up and carried on my shoulders, with his legs wrapped around my head, or even just on my hip, with his legs around my waist. I'd missed the whole important period in my youngest son's development, and nothing would ever bring it back. He'd be going into the first grade in September, and if I wasn't careful, he'd be graduating from high school before I knew it.

*I never intended to miss the most important years of my children's lives*, I thought, and then Jeremy's words hit me again. *Looking for a father.*

As we got back into the car, the children were asking one another if they would see any Indians when we got to Mexico. As we crossed the road into Tijuana and found the old road leading to Ensenada, I heard Mark Jr. say, "Let's ask Daddy; he knows everything!"

"Do you really know *everything*, Daddy?" Jeremy asked.

"Sometimes I do, son, and sometimes I don't."

"Then are we going to see any Indians?"

"We'll just have to wait and see, Jeremy. Sometimes that's the best way, just to wait and find out for yourself. Then you'll know the truth, not just because someone else told you it was true."

There were very few cars on the old road. Now and then, we would see a few people walking or a lone man on horseback. On the hillside to our left, a few houses dotted the landscape, and on our right, the ocean waves rolled gently along the sandy beach. Of course, the children wanted to get out and run along the shore, so we stopped at Rosarito Beach, which was practically deserted.

Betty spread a large blanket on the sand while the children took their shoes off and ran into the water, running back as soon as they put their toes in, then running out to try to catch the wave again.

"Let's just stay here forever," Betty said to me, getting the sand-wiches out of the picnic basket and stirring a large jar of homemade lemonade. "We'll let the children grow up wild on the beach, and they'll learn to fish and dig for clams and crabs. Then they'll support us in our old age, and we'll be carefree and happy beach bums for the rest of our lives."

I stretched out on the blanket, feeling the sun-warmed sand under my head and trickling through my toes. The sky was so blue and cloud-less overhead that I had to look at it through half-closed eyes, squinting at the sheer brightness all around me. I could taste the salt air deep in the back of my throat as I breathed it in, and I heard seagulls screech-ing in the distance, then saw them wheeling into the ocean for their dinner.

"Well," I said to Betty. "There is only one motel down the road, and I wouldn't mind having a bath right now and a real bed to sleep on. Otherwise, I'd be perfectly happy on the beach."

We ended up getting two adjoining rooms with a little kitchen-ette, parking our car right in front, all for three dollars a night. It was right across the street from the beach. Later that afternoon, we headed to the motel and parked. Two young boys came by and started to clean the car from bumper to bumper. It was really very nice of them, except that they were using dirty old rags and were smearing the car up so much with grease streaks that I said to them, "No, please don't clean our car. Here, I'll give you a quarter to watch it, okay? Whenever it's parked here, you just watch it. But promise not to clean it anymore, all right?"

Whenever we parked the car in our spot, the two little boys were there, standing by the car and watching it like guardian angels. If only I'd let them watch it instead of deciding to drive along the beach, I could have saved myself an awful lot of trouble.

We all thought it would be fun to take the car onto the sand, right along the water. It was fun, all right, but then we decided to go in for a swim, forgetting all about the car and having a ball. By the time we realized that the tide had been rolling steadily in toward the beach, we saw the waves were already washing up past the wheels of the car.

"You guys get up on the bank," I shouted. "I'll try and start the engine. Stand back, okay?"

The engine started well enough, but the car would not move, wouldn't budge at all, since it was firmly planted in the sand. The more I tried forcing it forward, the more deeply the tires worked themselves into the sand, digging in and entrenching themselves even deeper into the beach. I knew if I kept turning the engine, the chassis itself would finally come to rest on the sand like a great, beached whale.

As Betty and the children watched me with incredibly disappointed looks on their faces, I spotted three men on horseback approaching us. They were genuine vaqueros, with their riatas on their saddles, and I asked them in Spanish if they would kindly tie the riatas to the bumper of the car and pull it with their horses. They seemed pleased that I could converse with them, and I thought my luck had finally changed. So, with a bold gesture of overconfidence, I cried out, "All right, men. As soon as I give the signal, start to pull!"

Well, I gave the damned signal, and they started pulling all right, but the weight of the car was too much for their horses and riatas, and I heard them snapping almost as soon as I turned the key in the ignition.

The men were fuming mad at me, mumbling under their breaths and cursing me. They shook their heads defiantly, saying that I could take my car and throw it in the ocean, as they looped their riatas back on their saddles and rode off into the sunset, shaking their fists in the air.

I'd been watching the waves and studying them pretty carefully, and I noticed that every fifth one would roll all the way back, leaving enough space to drive the car onto the hard-packed wet sand as the tide pulled back. *If I could just get someone to help me roll the car up onto that little bank of hard sand*, I thought, *then we'd be home free.*

As luck would have it, I saw a lone ranch hand walking toward me. He said he would push the car toward the water whenever I told him to. As he got behind the car, I jumped in and started the engine. As I drove it forward, the wave rolled back. We slowly turned the car away from the water's edge. We were home free.

In ten minutes, this good man had helped me push the car back onto the roadway. It was an incredible job, and he deserved a lot of credit.

But I was more astonished when I suddenly heard a great round of applause break out. I thought at first that it must be the waves roaring in on the shore. As I turned my head to look up at the edge of the hill on the other side of the road, I saw a crowd of people waving and cheering as if to congratulate us on our achievement.

I wondered what the hell was going on. Had these people been watching us all along?

"I can't thank you enough, *señor*," I said to the ranch hand, reaching into my pocket to get my wallet out so I could give him a few dollars. But he wouldn't take anything and shook his head.

"I didn't do it for the money," he told me.

I looked at him and said, "I know, but you did so much work. You deserve something, *señor*."

"Just your thanks, that's sufficient," he replied, and we shook hands good-bye. I knew the man for only those fifteen minutes in my life, but I'll never forget him. It's amazing how a small act of kindness can stay in a man's mind all his life. I can only hope that something I've done, some small favor, has made a difference in someone else's life as well.

Betty and the kids thought we were terrific, saving their car. They told me I'd saved the day for them, as they were all worried that we would never be able to get home.

"Thanks," I told them, "and all those people watching us—I hope we gave them a good show, for free."

I learned not to take my car onto the beach anymore, but that was only the first lesson we learned in Mexico, because the next day, I decided to rent some horses for the family to go riding. Up until then, none of the others had ever been on a horse before. Betty and Dorothy decided to double up, although the vaquero wasn't sure it was a good idea. He was absolutely right, of course, since the horse began to buck as soon as my two favorite girls got on top of him.

The more he resisted having them on his back, the more tightly they held on to him for fear of falling off. They clamped their legs into his sides, sitting as stiffly as stones instead of trying to go with the flow of the horse's movements. For the next few minutes, we could hear them screaming for blocks around. By the time we caught up with them, grabbed the gelding's reins, and pulled him to a stop, Dorothy was in tears, and Betty said to me, "I really don't think I want to ride this horse anymore, Mark. Dorothy and I will just go swimming, if that's all right with you."

"Of course! You go swimming, honey. No one wants to force you into doing anything you don't want to do."

The boys were both laughing, as if watching them hold on for dear life was the funniest thing they'd ever seen. I thought the girls would just go down to the ocean and we'd meet them later on the beach, and I rode off with my two sons, who acted like cowpokes with years of experience.

Betty and Dorothy decided to have their swim in a swimming pool they'd noticed in a building across the street from the motel. Since other people were swimming there, they thought it would be perfectly okay for them to take their towels with them, putting their things under a lounge chair near the pool and diving in.

There was a large group of people standing around the pool. Some were drinking and balancing plates of food in one hand as they nibbled on various delicacies with the other. There was music in the air as well, and people were dancing to the music of a mariachi band when

Betty suddenly noticed that she and Dorothy were now the only ones in the pool.

As they looked around them, it slowly occurred to her that they had walked right into the middle of a large private party. Just as the idea dawned on her, it also seemed to dawn on the invited guests that perhaps this woman and her daughter hadn't been invited. Everyone gravitated toward the perimeter of the pool and stood there watching Betty and Dorothy standing motionless in the water.

"Isn't it all right for us to be here?" Betty asked one of the men smiling at her.

"Of course! It's all right," the man said, "although we maybe should introduce ourselves first."

He walked up to the side of the pool, crouched down, and told her his name. "We're just celebrating the opening of a new hotel and restaurant. You and your daughter are welcome to stay, of course."

Betty quickly got out of the pool, Dorothy right behind her, and they wrapped their towels around themselves. Betty said to the man, "I'm extremely sorry for having gate-crashed your private party. I would have never knowingly done it on purpose. Please forgive my terrible bad manners."

"There is nothing to forgive, dear lady. Please, be my guest, swim as much as you like, or come and join me at the buffet table, celebrate and drink with us. We are happy to have you both here with us today."

By this time, the boys and I were just finished with our long ride. I was incredibly saddle sore, since I hadn't been on a horse in ages. We were tired and dusty. When we didn't find the girls at the motel, we decided to cross the street to look for them.

I spotted them sitting around a table with a large sun umbrella sticking up through the middle, drinking iced sodas and eating their lovely salads with shrimp and avocados. My mouth started watering, and I headed straight for their table.

"You're sure living the high life," I said to Betty, thirsting for a cool drink and eyeing their glasses greedily. "Oh, please, won't you sit down and join us?" Betty said in her perfect British accent. "This is a private affair, but you are most welcome to draw up a chair and watch us eat this delicious food."

She started to laugh, explaining the whole story to me and boys. We all sat down to one of the nicest dinners I've ever had. I introduced myself to the hotel owner, and he was delighted to hear our various horseback-riding and car-drowning stories. We made friends with some of the most interesting people I had ever met.

It's always been amazing to me how easy it is to make friends when away from home, especially when on vacation, when we had no worries in the world except for a sore bottom and a somewhat soggy automobile. The way I felt that afternoon and evening, I would have taken any job in that hotel, should one have been offered, because I could have stayed there in Ensenada for the rest of my life.

It's always tempting to stay on vacation and never want to go home again. But the realities of my life were beginning to close in on me. We had to go home at the end of my leave.

When I reported back to March Air Force Base, I learned that my next assignment would be a permanent change of station, as a prison sergeant at the stockade of Andersen Air Force Base, on the island of Guam.

As an Air Force wife, Betty knew the routine well enough, but it was never easy for her, especially when I was sent away to a place where there was no immediate base housing for her and the children.

We lived apart from each other for a year after finding her and the children a furnished apartment in Richmond, California, and putting all our household goods in storage.

We said good-bye to each other in San Francisco. It was an awful moment for all of us. I hugged Betty, holding her as close to me as I could there in public. I could see the children huddled together behind her, holding on to one another for comfort. I kissed and held each one of them, telling them not to be sad, and asking them all to promise me they would take care of their mom for me.

"We promise, Daddy," they said in unison. "We promise," over and over again.

The sound of their voices kept getting smaller and smaller, and finally died out in the wind as I crossed the gangplank and finally boarded the USS *Barrett*, a troop ship operated by the Navy.

If I had known the conditions of the stockade where I was to spend the next three years, I might have jumped ship to swim all the way back to San Francisco.

# CHAPTER THIRTEEN

AFTER I'D MET my new commander in Guam and told him that I'd worked at San Quentin, he ordered me to gather up all my things and board the weapons carrier that would take me deep into the jungle where the stockade was located. As we got closer to the facility and I checked in with the confining officer, I saw what a terrible state the building was in, with rats and wild dogs eating trash everywhere around it.

"I'm going back to the base," the officer told me, "so you can take over now. I don't care how you run the place, as long as I don't hear any complaints about it."

He briefed me on my duties, and I noticed a lot of activity going on. When I asked him about it, he said they were getting ready for a double execution by hanging.

"They're flying the two condemned men in from Japan, since Guam is the nearest American soil in this part of the world."

Then I learned the entire story about these two soldiers who had raped and murdered a Guamanian woman on the Tamuning Highway near a disabled Sherman tank, way back in 1944 during the invasion of American forces in World War II.

They'd been filing one appeal after another after their court-martial and their sentencing to be hanged, but with no success. When I returned to my office, I saw the letter signed by President Truman, giving his regrets but instructing the installation commander to carry out the execution as quickly as possible.

The US Army flew in their hangman for the double execution. He was a regular soldier, a master sergeant who was a lot like the hangman of the Nazi war criminals at Nuremberg, Germany. He had ice-cold eyes that seemed to pierce right through mine when he looked at me.

When he came to the stockade and asked to see the prisoners, he told me he wanted to measure and weigh them. I escorted him to the black boxes where they were confined and felt a shiver run straight through me as he opened the door and went inside.

He was very courteous when he spoke to them, and before he left, he thanked them both. The officer on watch would sit on a chair outside the prisoners' boxes and just stare in at them for two hours at a time.

They were taken out separately every four hours to exercise for approximately twenty minutes. It was a grim detail, and on the day of the hanging, along with six of my men, I took them out of their cage-like boxes. We had handcuffed them with a restraining belt around their waists.

The intersections along the way were blocked off so that no one could disturb our convoy. The prisoners remained separate, since they would be hanged separately, with a long interval between them. As we approached the wooden scaffold, I went with the first prisoner, accompanied now by a preacher, and walked him up the ladder onto the platform where the hangman was waiting to put a hood over the man's head and quickly put the noose around his neck.

I could hear the prisoner praying as I walked down the ladder and took my place near the doctor who would pronounce the men legally dead. Everything went according to plan, the executioner doing his job quickly and efficiently, pulling the lever that tripped the door beneath the prisoner's feet. There was a horrible sound when the prisoner's neck broke, and I could hardly bear to watch the doctor make his examination and nod, saying, "Yes, this man is dead."

All I wanted to do was get the hell out of there. I'd seen executions before at San Quentin, but they seemed much more humane than this primitive, painful method of taking a man's life. Maybe they had committed a terrible crime, but I couldn't help wondering if there could have been a less painful way of carrying out justice to the condemned men. I almost felt like asking the hangman how he could do such a thing, how he could have spent his life doing it, but that's not a question that can be asked, and he probably would have said he did it because it was his job.

I had a job to do as well, getting rid of the huge rats and wild dogs and cleaning up the stockade. I decided to give the prisoners something to do; they were to catch the wild dogs so we could bring them to the vet, who would then put them to sleep with a simple injection. We made traps for the rats, and it became a never-ending chore, but eventually, after we'd cleaned the compound, there were fewer of them running under our feet all the time.

I had filed the appropriate forms to have my dependents brought over to live with me, and one fine day I was called into the orderly room and given the green light for family housing.

I can't describe the feeling that went through me at that moment, knowing that I wouldn't have to spend time without Betty and my children any longer.

I'd gotten to know the island pretty well in seven months, making friends with some of the islanders and even meeting a chieftain who practically owned a little village at the southern tip. He would take me and a few of the other men in his outrigger boats across the lagoon to Cocos Island, where we fished and went skin diving. I would have some beautiful places to show my family.

Guam was truly a beautiful place and really a paradise for children. There was a slow trade wind blowing most of the time, and it seemed to rain every twenty minutes or so. Since the temperature stayed at a constant eighty-five degrees all year round, no one ever minded the rain, and our clothes would be dry again in ten minutes or so.

After ten long months of feeling like a shipwrecked sailor, I was on my way home to pick up Betty and the children. When I landed at Travis Air Force Base, they were there to meet me, and it was an incredibly happy reunion.

"We just can't believe it," they all cried, "that we are really going back with you!"

"I know you'll all love it, even though it might take months for you to get used to scuba diving and fishing for lobsters and playing on the beach all the time. I know it will be hard for you to look for buried treasure on some out-of-the-way islands and play Tarzan by learning to swing from one tree to another on those long vines, and send out bloodcurdling yells to the animals, and—"

"Oh, Dad! Stop teasing us!" Mark Jr. said. "Be serious and tell us what it's really like!"

"Oh, but I am being serious, son. If you can't find real buried treasure, you can find plenty of old Army equipment all along the beaches. Dorothy, you can collect beautiful shells and study the coral that you see shining through the clearest blue water in the world. Betty, you and I can just sit and watch the most beautiful sunsets you've ever seen, while the kids tire themselves out with their fun and games."

I didn't know how I could be any luckier than I was at that moment. When we all boarded the USS *Barrett* together, on Christmas Eve 1954, I knew that I'd never be given a more wonderful Christmas present in all my life.

The most amazing part of our nineteen-day journey was the fact that we were given first-class accommodations in a five-berth cabin, so it was like a family cruise vacation for all of us and a second honeymoon for me and my beloved Betty.

As we crossed the international date line, we were delighted with the ceremonies, and the children all became members of the Order of the Dragon.

Unfortunately, when we arrived in Guam, we had to occupy temporary quarters at the Navy installation and were taken to a Quonset hut where we lived for the next two months in primitive, lizard-and-spider-infested rooms with torn screens at the windows and mosquitoes thick as paint on the ceilings.

The boys hardly noticed these little inconveniences, but it was tough on Betty and Dorothy, although they kept a stiff upper lip, in the true British/Basque form.

We were finally given excellent base housing, and my assignment was changed to Armed Forces Police, working in the capital city of Agana. I enjoyed riding with the Guamanian police, although they drove about ninety to one hundred miles per hour on emergency calls, which took some getting used to on the narrow roads.

The evenings were balmy and the beaches were frequently deserted. I'd often take the boys down to the beach to go snorkeling for lobster along the reef. We'd fill a large pot with salt water, then build a fire under it and let it come to a boil. Then I would put on my mask and flippers, diving into the lagoon and leaving my sons by the fire, always looking back toward the beach to make sure they were still there.

I was never afraid for their safety because it had never crossed my mind there was any real danger on the island, at least not until a local woman reported that she had seen a nearly naked Japanese soldier, who was wearing nothing but a sword and belt. Apparently, this old soldier had snuck up onto her porch, taking a handful of doughnuts that she had just baked and put outside on her window ledge to cool. She knew he was Japanese. Although she didn't understand anything that he said, she recognized the language well enough.

I contacted the Navy base, and they dispatched a dozen Marines to help me search for the man. We searched the jungles and even the beach, but we never did find him. Later, a Japanese soldier gave himself up to the American patrol group, telling the intelligence officer during an interview that he and some other surviving Japanese soldiers had been instructed never to surrender. He was unaware that the war had ended and had been living in the jungle and going to the beaches late at night to catch fish to survive.

If I'd known that any Japanese soldiers were still alive and living in the jungles, I would never have taken my boys and left them on the deserted beaches at night. Within two months we rounded up three surviving Japanese soldiers. They gave us no resistance. They just wanted to go home to their families, like all old soldiers want to do.

I volunteered to become Cub Scout master for all the Air Force kids on Andersen AFB. When the Little League baseball season opened, I became manager of one of the teams. Betty acted as den mother and found a job at the bank on base. We were all pulling together, and we started saving some money. I wanted to keep my promise to Betty and the kids and be able to send her home to see Nan the following year.

We were invited to a luau by the chieftain and his villagers and ate something we thought was chicken but turned out to be coconut crabs. These were the ugliest creatures on earth, but that was my opinion. They were crabs with thick black hairy fur on their backs, and they had protruding faces that looked like bats.

Betty picked up something from the table that she also thought was chicken and was so delighted that she made a point to go up to the hostess and say, "I just love this chicken. Will you please give me the recipe?"

"Why, certainly," the woman said, grinning broadly. "But it isn't chicken, you know. It's banana bat!"

"Banana what?" Betty asked, and as soon as the hostess confirmed that the meat had indeed been fried bat, Betty said, "Uh, excuse me," and ran as fast as her legs would carry her to the nearest ladies' room.

We outlived a terrible typhoon and became used to going to the base's open-air theater in the evening, all huddled up under a poncho during the rain while watching the movie. We had no television on the island and we had no windowpanes, as our base housing only had screens and louvers. We didn't get too many fresh eggs, or fresh produce either, as everything had to be flown into the base from the United States. But sometimes we were lucky, when a flight crew would go to Japan and bring back cases of the precious stuff, which would be rationed out on a first come, first serve basis.

I survived my training for the sea-rescue squad, learning to dive to the bottom of the reef with an Aqua-Lung on my back, and then exchanging the lung with another swimmer, still on the bottom, doing so without inhaling any water.

The rescue squad was formed because every time a bomber wing came over on a ninety-day temporary duty, one or two airmen were occasionally washed off the coral reefs into the undertow. Although we were called out to search for them, it would have taken a miracle to rescue them, as they were probably lost forever.

When my assignment in Guam was coming to an end, I found out that I could have consecutive overseas tours, which meant I could apply for an assignment in England. This was the best news Betty could have heard, since she would be reunited with her grandmother.

We decided on the spot that we would get all the paperwork completed, and with many complications and delays along the way, we finally made it to England in September 1956. Going from Agana, Guam, to London, England, was like being part of man's evolution from prehistoric times right into the present. We were stationed at West Drayton Royal Air Force station, near Heathrow Airport, and everything we could possibly have wanted, everything in the development of civilized man, was now at our doorstep. We rented a large house in Windsor not far from the famous castle and settled down to an active family life.

It seems a man's life is like a mountain range; there are high points and low points, with long stretches in between level planes. If I were to chart the progression of my life, I would have to say that my years in England were the happiest, on the most even terrain, situated in my memory halfway from beginning to end. It was a time of rest and recuperation from the past and a jumping-off point to the future, with all the great sadness and sorrow that was still to come but was yet unknown.

Perhaps it was a good thing that I didn't know in advance what was in front of me. If I had, I might not have had the courage to face it. I might have tried to hide from it instead, especially finding myself in the most civilized, law-abiding, cultural city in the world.

I would have done anything to keep us in London because the four-year tour of duty wasn't long enough to do all the things we wanted to do.

Those years were the best, by far, of my twenty-four-year career in the Air Force, and the only thing that was wrong with them was their shortness, like the blinking of an eye.

If I only had twenty-four hours to live, my stay in London would have narrowed itself down to a single minute, to the taking of a few short breaths, happy breaths, to a dream that faded all too quickly from my memory.

Our years in England were really Betty's years. She'd been only a girl when she left, but she was fully a woman now, a wife and mother, a professional secretary, and even the chairwoman of the entertainment committee of the NCO Wives Club. She also volunteered to take over the Teen Club functions, taking the young members into London to see stage shows and acting as their chaperone. Her greatest accomplishment with the teenagers was when she took them to Paris, which involved chartering a plane, making hotel accommodations, and booking all their sightseeing tours. She always managed to keep the group together, and sometimes the boys and I would accompany her and the group. It amazed me how she always returned all the kids home safely.

Nan, of course, was our greatest delight, spending weeks at a time with us in Windsor and enjoying herself with her great-grandchildren. She was a very special person in Betty's life, and I could see why as I watched them converse and laugh together at little things that had happened during Betty's growing-up years.

Each time Betty drove to London to pick up her grandmother, Nan would always have presents for the children and both Betty and me. When Christmas rolled around, we entertained all Nan's sisters and their families at our house for several days, enjoying the delicious food each would bring with them and the special dinners Betty would so lovingly prepare. I was indeed a fortunate man, being accepted into such a wonderful family, a family I truly loved.

Betty became reacquainted with her father. We spent many weekends at his beach house on Canvey Island, where we rode horses and went out into the sea at high tide to look for seashells. He owned a confectioner's shop, selling newspapers and magazines, ice cream and candy. Jeremy and Mark Jr. loved to visit his little store. They would spend half an hour trying to decide exactly how to spend the prized half crowns we had given them.

Our children were precious to us, but Betty and I were delighted when we were able to plan a two-week vacation, leaving the children at home. We went with another couple to Palma de Mallorca, one of the Spanish Balearic Islands in the Mediterranean.

We did the usual amount of sightseeing, which always tired me out. But the countryside was so lyrically beautiful, and I felt so close to my own Basque roots somehow, that I couldn't see enough of the island. I wanted to keep going or go dancing and drinking long after the others were entirely exhausted and ready for a good night's sleep.

*Who needs sleep when you're on one of the most beautiful islands in the world?* I thought while tossing and turning in my bed, knowing that Spain itself, my father's homeland, was only a short plane trip away. I could almost feel it right outside our window.

We stopped in Madrid on our way back, making a special point to visit the street that bore my grandfather's name, my name! Even though Betty had only married into my family, she was so proud that she stopped one of the Guardia Civil on the street and said, "That's our name on the street sign. See?" He looked at her in such a strange way that I had to come to her rescue and explain what in the world she was raving about.

One fine morning, we decided to rent Lambretta scooters and drive all the way to the other side of the island and take a tour through the Drach Caves (Cuevas del Drach), the famous caves that were used by Arab pirates to stash their plundered loot, and even though it was a typical tourist trap, I was deeply moved by the experience. I let my imagination run away with me, conjuring up all kinds of romantic images as we wandered through the dark and damp caves.

On our way back to the hotel, my rear wheel came off the Lambretta. Betty went careening one way, and I, still on the scooter, went the other. Betty hit the pavement and landed on her head as I rolled for another fifty yards. Luckily for us, another couple stopped their car to pick us up. They took us back to the hotel, where Betty was immediately examined by a doctor, who said she was just fine.

It's funny how we could meet people accidentally on vacation and end up having a really great time with them. These Good Samaritans invited us to the bullfight the next afternoon. As we joined them in our seats, we were able to spend an hour or so watching and studying all the people around us, and then experiencing our first bullfight.

From our vantage point in the arena, we could see very clearly the Spanish upper class, sitting right below us in all their Sunday best, wearing hats and gloves even though it was quite warm. In the next row above the Spaniards, some Englishmen and women were sitting, also dressed to kill.

After the featured matador entered the ring, the crowd got to their feet, cheering as enthusiastically as any American football or baseball fan would, their cheers all blending together as one.

I was enthralled at every movement the matador made, waving his cape into a full veronica and twirling around on his toes like a ballerina, except that he was an incredibly brave man, in spite of his grace and the colorful decorations on his costume.

When the time came to actually kill the bull, the matador stood straight and tall, carefully aiming his sword, and as the bull made its final charge, the matador drove his sword to the hilt right into the bull's shoulders. There was an unbelievable amount of spurting blood, like a minor volcano erupting, and when the animal began coughing up his own blood, one of the English ladies stood, leaned over, and threw up all over the finely dressed Spanish noblemen and women in front of her.

It was an awful sight, combined with the death of the bull, which had kneeled in the middle of the arena and then toppled over. We couldn't help it; we all started laughing at the same time, and then everyone on either side of us was laughing with us. We were all caught up in the spectacle of the blood and lust, mixed with cultural refinement.

Much to my dismay, we didn't have time to visit the Basque Country, but I had now been to Spain, even to Madrid and Barcelona, seeing my grandfather's name just as he had told me I would. I felt proud as I sat on the plane that would take us back to London.

My tour of duty had ended in England. Betty was crying as we drove from Nan's house after saying our final good-bye. "I just know I'll never see her again," she said through her sobs. "I feel so guilty leaving her all alone. I couldn't talk her into coming back with us, Mark. She won't leave her beloved England, you know."

The following week we were on a plane heading for the United States. My next assignment was in the wilds of Larson Air Force Base, where the nearest town was Moses Lake, Washington, in the great northwest USA.

It was really a hunter's haven, especially pheasant hunting in the valley farms, and the elk and deer in the mountains were plentiful. There was wonderful fishing in the Columbia River, which was always full of salmon and trout and an occasional sturgeon.

I never got closer to the wild than when I took my sons hunting the next year. I also got closer to my two boys during our hunting trips, which we all called safaris. It was a special time for us, a time each of us would remember through our lifetimes. They even bagged a bear with my .338 Magnum, which had three tons of striking energy and a nine-power scope. They got it in the upper torso and brought it down with only one round.

I did some more hunting a few years later, when I was sent to Vietnam, although it wasn't the kind of safari I'd always dreamed of. Many things happened in my life between then and my tour of duty in Phan Rang; we had moved to New Hampshire, then to Torrance, California, where I became an Air Force recruiter.

My sons were thinking about going to college, both making first string in wrestling and football at the local high school. My daughter, Dorothy, had married a local man from Moses Lake, Washington, son of a wealthy farmer and cattleman. I was even expecting my first grandchild. I wasn't happy about her marriage, but everything seemed to pale by comparison after being in Vietnam. I needed to get these experiences out of my system, by writing about them and exorcising the old ghosts that have haunted me all these years.

I had been following the news about the United States and the involvement in Vietnam for about a year, hoping all along that I wouldn't have to go, since I felt that the north and south were fighting a civil war. I felt we had no business sending our soldiers to die in that country. Even so, in the fall of 1966, I was called in to my commander's office, and he gave me notice that I would be shipping out; I didn't like it. Notwithstanding, I remained calm.

Betty was furious, saying over and over again how unfair it was, but that was only the first stage in the full range of emotions she went through before I shipped out. First the anger, then the coolheaded acceptance of the facts, which then changed into an almost longing for me to come back, even before I'd left.

I didn't think it was fair, and I got angry, then felt sorry for myself. I was miserable for days, thinking that I was too old at forty-eight to be soldiering in Vietnam and yet still too young to die. It wasn't even dying, necessarily, that I was concerned about, but having to live for a year in the jungle, fighting Vietcong, snakes, and diseases of all kinds.

I decided to have a long talk with my boys to make sure they'd take good care of their mother, whether or not I made it back.

"We'll take care of her, Dad, don't worry," they both said to me. "You can trust us one hundred percent."

They were almost too big to hug, but I did it anyway. Then Jeremy looked up at me and said, "We'll know how to handle things. After all, we're your sons, Dad. You had to take care of your mom when you were still a kid, but look at us! We're not kids anymore. Hell, we're all grown up, Dad!"

All grown? Well, even if they weren't, I knew they would learn to be soon enough if I didn't come back from another war, this time in Vietnam.

# CHAPTER FOURTEEN

I CAN STILL remember the shock I felt at my first sight of Phan Rang, situated in the midlands, near the South China Sea. It was hardly more than a clearing in the jungle. We had to build our hootches first, and it should have been easy to throw them up, but the lumber at hand was solid mahogany, wood so hard that we could barely drive a nail through it. It was obvious why it was called ironwood.

Starting with just a few tents, we worked as quickly as we could, building mortar bunkers and our living quarters. When the troops began arriving, we weren't prepared to house everyone. We weren't prepared for the scorpions, snakes, and tigers either.

As we cleared the land, the whole earth rebelled. Creatures slithered and crawled around everywhere. We were changing the ecological structure of the country, and since no one bothered to hunt tigers anymore, their population just kept increasing.

We had to get used to seeing cobras, which would slither into the area looking for a warm spot to sleep. Whenever we had to go into the bunkers, we'd have to grab the scorpions by their tails, chop their heads off, and toss them over the top. I stepped on one in the shower one morning, and it stung me so badly that I limped for a week.

We noticed the native women working their rice paddies, and how they would leave their infants lying on a nearby bank. The tigers would sneak up to the baby, grab it by the head, and carry the infant off into the jungle.

My buddy and I wanted to catch a tiger or two, so we made a couple of baby dummies, sprayed them with milk, and left them by the bank as we hid with our loaded M16s in camouflage uniforms under a poncho. We tried to explain it all to the *mamasans*, but they had no idea what we were trying to convey to them. The tigers weren't fooled one bit, because we never did see one get anywhere near our dummies. The very next day, another baby disappeared from the same rice paddy. It made me sick at heart, and it had nothing to do with the war itself.

If it wasn't the tigers, it was the king cobra that was a threat to our lives, without the enemy's help. The snakes were responsible for hundreds of deaths in Southeast Asia, and they were everywhere, along with smaller, deadly snakes. The python, the largest snake, however harmless, can squeeze the life out of a man and took three men to move.

I had a near fatal experience with a cobra one morning on my way to see the new arrivals. I was near the bomb dump where some forklifts were parked. I came face-to-face with the cobra, all curled up, practically at my feet. As the snake started to coil upward, standing straight upright, it unfolded its hood and tried to stare me down, as if to see which one of us would move or die first. It seemed like an eternity waiting; I was hardly breathing at all. I prayed, "Dear God, I'll do anything if you'll get this cobra out of here!"

If bitten, I would certainly die within minutes; I'd seen it happen to a man. The cobra was still attached by its fangs to the man's leg as we all stood by watching helplessly.

Suddenly, the snake slowly lowered its body to the ground and deflated its hood. I was stiff all over with fear, but I managed to shout at some kids approaching me, warning them to stay clear of the forklift because of the cobra.

"Start the lift! Run over the damned snake!" someone was yelling back at me. I managed to run over it, but all it did was raise and lower itself, biting in a futile gesture at the impervious tire that was pinning it down.

I was assigned to a munitions squadron, responsible for storing and loading bombs and ammunition onto the jets. We also made napalm, a mixture of low-grade jet fuel and detergent, which killed its victims not only by severely burning them but also suffocated them to death, as the napalm literally burned up the available oxygen for a thousand feet from its ignition point.

I had to close my eyes to a lot of things that were bothering me, had to be deaf, dumb, and blind sometimes, just to save my sanity. But I could never completely block things out of my mind. They remained there, tucked away in the back, and they sometimes inched their way forward, sometimes hitting me over the head when I least expected it— like the water buffalo that charged us once and almost got us killed.

That's the funny part, but it's only funny as I look back. While it was charging straight at me, I didn't think it was the least bit humorous. What I mean is this: In the middle of all the fighting and killing, I was almost wiped out by a mean-looking cow.

Another guy and I were on our way to the bomb dump; it was just a narrow path for hauling munitions to the flight line. We could hardly see the animals at first in the head-high bushes, but we heard them and then noticed the babies, or calves. I had a gut feeling right away about these buffalo, and I told my buddy to make sure his M16 was loaded.

"Aw, don't be afraid of them!" he said to me in his southern accent. "My God, they're just cows, for Christ's sake! They're as tame as puppy dogs."

I had grown up around cattle, and I knew these animals weren't puppy dogs, no matter how tame they usually were. As we rounded a small hill, halfway between our hootches and the dump, we spotted a dozen or so just down the pathway.

"See?" my buddy said. "They won't bother us. They're just as tame as can be. What did I tell you?"

No sooner had he gotten those words of wisdom out of his mouth than the herd turned around and came to a stop about a hundred yards away from us. Then they turned again. They were digging their heels into the ground. It reminded me of the bull in Palma de Mallorca just before it charged. Sure enough, the cows lowered their heads and came barreling toward us at full speed like a freight train.

There were no convenient trees around for us to climb, and the brush on the side of the pathway was too thick for us to penetrate. I pumped a round into the chamber of my M16 and got down on one knee, aiming over their heads and firing two rounds into the air.

My buddy was already in a panic as the cows picked up speed. He ran off toward the hootches and I could hear him hollering and carrying on as loud as he could.

Then I aimed directly at one of the cows, hitting it right between the eyes as the rest of them scattered. It was so close to me at that very moment that I could have shaken hands with it. The cow turned a somersault about five feet in front of me and I made the sign of the cross over my chest and thanked God for coming to my rescue.

Hearing the shots, a bunch of guys came driving down the narrow pathway, expecting to find the Vietcong. After seeing it was just a dead cow, they went back for a truck and a hoist, loaded the cow into the back, and drove it back to camp, butchered the animal, and refrigerated hundreds of pounds of meat. We had barbecues for days afterward.

One day, I was comparing combat notes with a young second lieutenant by the name of Potter. We got into a debate about air combat versus combat on the ground. As a company commander, he obviously thought his own point of view was the right one.

"I'll tell you what. You can't compare two things unless you know them both," he advised me. "I'm going on a search-and-destroy mission in the next few days. Why don't you come with me and find out about combat for yourself?"

"Sure, I'll be happy to tag along," I told him. "I'll get permission from the squadron commander."

When I went to speak with Captain Henry, he said it was okay with him, providing we took him along too. Lieutenant Potter said he had no objections to bringing us both and instructed us to take only our rifle, four clips of ammo, a bayonet, and a canteen full of water.

We got into the waiting trucks and drove all day into the mountains, stopping just before sundown. In that part of the world, the word *sundown* means exactly that; as soon as the sun sets, the night is as black as a hole, especially when there's no moon.

"Stay close to the man in front of you," Potter said.

I took one last look at the terrain around us, seeing nothing but high mountains and thick forests. By the time the sun was down, I could hardly see my hand in front of my face, let alone the man directly in front of me. I had to reach out and touch him to know he was still right there.

I said one Hail Mary and got in line in front of the captain, following the lieutenant as he started to climb the mountain. We were going almost straight up and had to stop every ten feet for a rest. Then we would descend a few feet, and it was almost impossible to keep our balance, since we never knew from one minute to the next what the lay of the land would be just in front of us.

The air was hot and sultry, making it impossible to stay dry. We were drenched in sweat and seemed to be breathing water vapor. I couldn't figure out how the lieutenant navigated his way through the mountain, but at daybreak we found ourselves in what he said was a village, although the trees were so thick that it was hard to see anything but forest all around us. The plants were steaming in the morning light, and by this time, we could squeeze out our clothing like sponges and feel the water dripping down to our feet.

When the valley opened up in front of us, we saw something moving, running in the distance, and the lieutenant shouted, "Take cover and hold your fire!"

I said to myself, *Well, this is it, Vergara! Sooner or later, either the Vietcong, the animals, or a tropical disease will get us all.* I honestly felt as if we were all living on borrowed time. Now I was really going to find out what the infantry went through in hand-to-hand combat.

A squad was sent out to the front. They were gone for a long time, but when they returned, all they brought with them was an old, ancient-looking couple, all alone and scared to death. Apparently, they were the only survivors in the village, both left behind to die.

"Well, let's bring them along with us," Potter said to the Vietnamese scout, who told the old couple what was being said.

They mumbled something to him, and he translated. "They want to stay here," he said, shrugging his shoulders. "They've never left their home before, and they don't know anything about the war. They don't even know who's on which side. They just want to be left alone."

"Well, we can't leave them here," Potter told him. "They'll slow us down a bit, but they've got to come with us. Tell them."

I never did see what had happened in the village. The lieutenant wanted us all to get out of there as quickly as we could. It took us what seemed like an eternity to get back to our base, and I was happy to get back to my hootch and my own bed, even though I didn't see any action. I never saw the lieutenant again, although I later learned that he was killed at Pleiku.

Maybe I should have stayed right where I was, but a few weeks later, I joined Sam Stevens, a new friend of mine, on a trip to Da Lat, a mountain town that had once been a resort during the French occupation. Sam's commander was a pilot who flew the C-47, or Gooney, assigned to the base, and he agreed to take us there.

Our pilot had some trouble landing on the very short runway, and we started tumbling down the other side of the mountain after his first unsuccessful attempt to land. But he was a seasoned flier, pushing the throttles forward until he got up enough speed to become airborne again. This time he brought us to the ground with full flaps down.

Sam and I got down the mountain. We took a cab into town and found a hotel room for the night. We went straight back out again into the marketplace, and for the first time, I saw the Vietcong walking right out in the open, armed to the teeth.

Even though the town itself hadn't been bombed, the scars of war were visible in all the people's faces. Some of them were badly crippled, walking on all fours and begging in the streets. I had to swallow these sights and sounds without letting them break me down or else there's no way I could have survived the mental anguish of just being a witness to the destruction, physical as well as emotional.

Sam and I found ourselves a restaurant. It was filled with well-dressed men and women and generals with medals on their chests, surrounded by young girls. There were quite a few American men and women, and Sam and I suspected they were all CIA operatives. We had a couple of drinks but spoke to no one, retiring early to our hotel.

The next morning, we took a walk through the streets where the rich French merchants and farm owners had lived in great mansions, some of them bigger than any of the fanciest homes I'd seen in Beverly Hills. Sadly, they were all boarded up and abandoned. I was surprised that the peasants hadn't moved into them or that the Vietcong hadn't turned them into their headquarters. But that's not the kind of war we were fighting, and our enemy, which normally kept itself invisible, definitely wasn't the Nazi army of occupation.

We stopped at the home of the Christian mission and met the American director, whose name was Anna. She was the most marvelous, intelligent, self-effacing, and yet enormously talented woman I think I have ever met, speaking fluent Vietnamese and a Montagnard dialect, among many others. She offered us tea and cookies, and I naïvely asked her if she'd ever encountered the Vietcong.

"Oh yes," she said, smiling. "Every time I go into the mountains to visit the villagers. I see them on the road all the time."

I was going to ask her if she wasn't afraid, but it seemed like a silly question.

"And do they ever bother you or threaten you in any way?"

"They know who I am," she answered, quite nonchalantly. "They know I'm trying to help their people, so why should they bother me?"

Then just for the hell of it, I said, "Can I go with you on your next trip to the mountains?"

Sam gave me a queer look but then said, "Hey, I'd like to come along too. What the hell? Oh, excuse me, please!"

Anna laughed and said it was all right with her and that she wouldn't mind having two big, strong men to accompany her. "We can go tomorrow, if you like. But leave your military IDs at the hotel, and don't bring anything along that would mark you as soldiers."

At daybreak on the following morning, Anna picked us up in her Land Rover, driving surely and quickly in a southeasterly direction from Da Lat. The road was narrow in some parts and quite steep. There was thick jungle everywhere, with monkeys and birds peeping out of the tree branches. Every once in a while, a deer would cross our path, and when we got to the first village and parked the car, there were suddenly people everywhere. They gracefully stepped to one side to let us pass. Anna seemed to know many of them on sight, saying something indistinctly and quietly, making it difficult for us to hear, either in Vietnamese or in their mountain dialect.

At one point, she looked down and said to us, under her breath, "Be careful and don't say anything. Those are VC approaching us, so just smile and wave to them."

Smile and wave at the VC, our enemy? I wasn't about to ask any questions at that point, especially since Sam and I were unarmed and in the company of a lady missionary, so we both did as she said.

They were dressed in black linen, wearing red bandanas around their foreheads. They were each carrying two bandoliers crisscrossed over their chests, ammo belts around their waists, a rifle and machete, and some were even carrying parts of a machine gun and large ammo boxes, so they were like walking ammunition depots.

Anna kept smiling at them and talking to them as if they were some nice old ladies she was meeting at a social function. I had to pretend that I could make out everything they were saying, but it made my skin crawl, and I could almost feel the hair on my head and chest turning white because I knew they could see that my friend and I weren't ministers of the peace. I clenched my jaws together and acted like a happy idiot until they turned the corner and were out of sight.

It was time to get on to the next village, where Anna was going to tend to some sick children. When we got to the first house, there were so many babies in the crib that she found one lying perfectly still among the other crying infants.

"This baby is dead," she said to one of the many women in the room, but it didn't seem to make any difference to any of them. After we left, I asked Anna why they hadn't done anything about the child's body.

"They told me they knew the baby was dead," she answered me, with a look of great sadness in her eyes. "They said they would get around to burying it, sooner or later. The baby was a girl, so it didn't matter much to them. A baby girl in this country is just a burden to her parents, since it will never grow up to be a soldier and learn to kill the enemy."

She wouldn't let us wander through the villages and touch anything. She wore long rubber gloves since she was treating people with diseases that were unknown to the outside world.

"Until this war is over," she said, "they can't be treated properly, and even then, it will take years to heal them and a certain amount of miracle working."

When we stopped at another village for dinner, Sam, who also spoke French fluently, cornered some Vietnamese and convinced them that it would be all right to speak French with us, even though they were forbidden to speak it after the French had been kicked out. We were invited to spend the evening with them and had a good, long talk with Anna, who explained to us that she had been a missionary for almost twenty years.

"I've been in Africa and most of Southeast Asia, and in South America as well. I had to leave the Amazon Indians in Brazil because the government had authorized the Army to kill them as well as destroy their villages. It was terribly hard to go, since I knew that the people and their way of life were being wiped out."

"Why you?" I asked her as we talked on through the night. "Why did you become a missionary?"

"Oh, that's easy," she replied. "I believe in the word of God, and I am needed, even sought after, if that doesn't sound too vain, by a number of religious groups since I pick up languages so quickly. Just like that," she continued, and she snapped her fingers.

On our return to Da Lat the next day, we stopped at four more villages, where Anna changed bandages and gave out more pills and medical instructions. We finally got back to our hotel just as the sun was going down.

Anna was an inspiration to us both. After meeting her, Sam and I decided that we would do something, no matter how small, to help an orphanage, perhaps. We had heard about one that had been set up near an old French Catholic church not too far from our base in Phan Rang.

# CHAPTER FIFTEEN

SAM AND I had no trouble making our way back to our base. In fact, we both felt extremely lucky, having left Da Lat without being detained by the Vietcong, or worse, being killed in our beds at the hotel.

"It had to be Anna," Sam said to me. "With the influence that woman has, it had to be because of her that we are both still alive, Mark."

"You could be right, Sam," I answered, thinking of the close call we had with the Vietcong only a day or so earlier. "You have to admit, she was some kind of woman."

"Yeah, she was that all right. It takes some kind of woman to do the things she does, lots of guts, but then if you have been doing it for almost your entire life, it wouldn't be hard, would it?"

"I guess not. It's never hard spending your life helping others. Say, Sam, what about that orphanage? Let's mosey on down there and see if we can help out, shall we? We can do it in remembrance of Anna."

"In honor of Anna, you mean. Sure, Mark, who knows, we may even like helping out the kids. It will be something to do in our spare time. So, yeah, I'm game."

On the next Sunday morning, Sam and I checked out a truck, and with a few of the guys, we all went looking for the orphanage. When we found the priest, we assured him that we only wanted to help the kids. He asked us if we had any whiskey.

"Sure," I said, looking at the guys and hoping one of them had a bottle with them. We gave him the whiskey, and when the priest put it to his lips, we thought he'd never stop drinking.

He wiped his mouth on his shirtsleeve, smiled a great big grin, and said, "Now I'll show you to the orphanage, boys. You are truly fine men; I can see it as plain as the nose on my face!"

I didn't think he'd be able to see his own nose, let alone mine, but he seemed to perk up and was now being a lot more friendly, especially after he finished the bottle.

The building was surrounded by a six-foot wall, in the French style, and was operated by a very old Vietnamese nun, who looked extremely tired and worn-out. There must have been thirty children there, ranging in age from babies in arms to preteenagers. Ninety percent of them were girls, and I couldn't help thinking that their relatives, if they still had any alive, had found the best place to get rid of them.

As we tried talking to the old nun, some of the children came running to tell her that someone had just left another baby at the gate. We followed her to the entrance and there, wrapped in a dirty blanket, lay another baby girl. One of the airmen picked her up and brought her back to the main building, where he washed her and put her down in a makeshift box. He then drove off in the truck and was gone for about an hour, returning with some milk and whatever food the base cook would let him have.

At first the children wouldn't come anywhere near the American food. I'm sure they had never seen canned tomatoes or green beans before. They couldn't figure out what to do with the plastic-wrapped bags of corn chips and potato chips. They felt the food through the bags and laughed with one another, then shrugged their shoulders as if it were all beyond them. But hunger knows no barriers, and soon they had finished it all. Sam and I fed the milk to the babies in their makeshift bassinets, all except for one, who had died.

The nun said nothing. She picked up the baby and wrapped some cloths around its body, saying something to a teenage boy, who then put the dead child in a handmade box. We went with her as she took the box to the end of the yard, where several holes had already been dug, as if in preparation for the dying or deceased.

As the box was lowered in the ground, the nun said a few words and told us she was grateful we had noticed the dead body, since they must be buried quickly to prevent the spread of disease.

From then on, we visited the orphanage every week. We got them GI blankets, wall lockers, tables, and food. I wrote Betty a letter telling her all about it. She began collecting clothes from the neighborhood, getting the local PTA and high school involved. We received dozens of packages filled with clothes, medicine, and vitamins. My letters must have touched her heart because she organized the entire neighborhood into gathering all kinds of needed supplies. Every night Betty would wash, sew, box, and wrap the items herself, take them to the post office, and pay the postage herself.

One day I went to the base doctor. I asked him if he could come and examine some of the children. He said he'd be happy to and brought two medics with him. He found that many babies had tuberculosis, explaining they didn't have much longer to live. He gave most of them shots and left with a very heavy heart.

The older nun we had met the first day expired and was replaced by two younger nuns. When the doctor came back to the orphanage for another visit, he helped train the two young women in some simple, basic medical care. The old priest was also replaced by a much younger man, and we were influential in finding jobs on the base for a few of the teenage orphans.

Since Sam Stevens and I were among the first men to arrive in Phan Rang, we were the first who were eligible for R & R. We chose to visit Hong Kong and caught a Pan Am flight from Cam Ranh Air

Base. After landing, we decided to spend our first week in Hong Kong itself. We would then go to Kowloon, across from Hong Kong Island, since we had heard that was where all the action was.

Old Sam and I got a little more action than we had expected. Sam really wasn't that old to begin with; he was in his thirties, but he had the face of a much older man. He was just a slow-moving, lazy kind of guy. Born and raised in Kansas wheat country, he had never seen the ocean until his enlistment in the Air Force. He was now seeing the world, including the lowest, dirtiest, and most corrupt underworld.

One day, after we felt completely rested and at ease, happy to be alive, our curiosity took us to what was called Sin City, an underground opium den. We had been strongly advised not to go there, as neither of us definitely was the opium-smoking type. We weren't interested in buying marijuana or trying hard drugs, but we went anyway for the fun of it, or so we thought.

It was an underground labyrinth of corridors leading into tiny rooms with bunk beds along the wall and people lying around in a thick blue haze, smoking every weed known to man. If we had been looking for a murderer, pusher, or thief, we could have found them there by the dozen. They actually had one policeman patrolling, but his main job was to get the beggars and punks out of the way so that the dope smokers could walk in and out as they pleased. We were told by the policeman at the front gate that there were only two ways to get in and out of Sin City.

"Some of these people never see the light of day once they come inside," he said. "Once they get hooked on the opium, their complexion turns yellow and they lose their interest in food, which means losing weight and lying down for days, hardly moving at all. A few get belligerent at seeing us standing around and try to pick a fight, sometimes pulling out a good-size switchblade."

I poked Sam's elbow and said, "We'd better be getting out of here before someone decides to kill us for no good reason. Okay?"

"I'm with you," Sam agreed, but as soon as we tried to find the entrance, we started going around in circles. Every hallway seemed to lead us into a dead end, or else we would wind up back where we started. My heart began to pump extra fast as I wondered if we'd ever get outside again. All I wanted to do was find the policeman, who had at least been polite enough to talk with us without drawing a weapon.

Sam then made the huge mistake of asking some dopeheads for the way out; all they did was give us a great big grin. We got you now! their eyes seemed to be saying. Now you'll wish you never came here in the first place!

I whispered to Sam, "If anyone tries anything, let's just stand back-to-back and work our way out like we're attached to each other."

Finally, help arrived in a little kid who ran up to us and said, "Me know how to get out. You gimme five dollars, Hong Kong money, okay, GI?"

"Okay, sure, kid," I said, "but you show us the way out first, and then we'll give you the five dollars, Hong Kong. Okay?"

"Okay!" he said, signaling us to follow him. We should have known better; as soon as he started going down some more stairs, winding deeper and deeper underground, I realized he was leading us right into a trap. When we got to the bottom of the stairs, there were half a dozen punks blocking the way.

"Going somewhere, Yankee?" asked the biggest punk, extending his hand, palm up, for me to grease it with some money.

"I sure am," I yelled. Then I summoned my courage and all my vocal powers and shouted, "This is it. It's now or never, Sam." As I was about to plunge into the crowd of thugs and fight my way out, the policeman showed up and ordered everybody to get out of our way.

I was never so happy to see the blue sky again and to breathe in the fresh air. We didn't go back to Sin City. We spent the rest of our time at the expensive but perfectly normal Hilton Hotel on Hong Kong

Island, where hundreds of other normal Americans and English people were spending their vacations above the ground.

Normal people—although that is sometimes a difficult judgment to make about even the nicest people you meet.

An Englishman introduced himself to us at the bar. He told us he was a recent widower, and his home was in Hunstanton, England.

"What a small world," I said, looking at him. "My daughter was born in Hunstanton in 1944. My wife is British, that is, by birth; she's an American citizen now, by choice, that is, although not from Norfolk; we were stationed there after I finished my missions at Thurleigh."

He was so surprised and pleased hearing about Dorothy being born in his hometown that he invited us for drinks, saying that it would be his pleasure to buy Sam and me dinner.

Sam and I were delighted to spend time with this man. He was a retired colonel of the British army who had served in the Burma campaign during the Second World War. His son was with the government in Hong Kong, and he invited us to a dinner party at his son's house the following evening.

We got the idea that it would be a fancy party, and we decided to each have a suit made in the marketplace of Kowloon. There were advertisements everywhere in the hotel telling guests they could be measured for a suit at one in the afternoon, and it would be delivered to the guest by five the same evening. The price was right for us, and *What the hell*, we thought, neither one of us had worn a suit of civilian clothes in ages; even when we went to Da Lat, we only wore slacks and white open-necked shirts. Sure enough, just before five o'clock our suits were delivered. They fit perfectly.

The colonel's son lived above the Central District, on Hong Kong Island. We had to cross over on the Star Ferry from Victoria Harbour and then get a cab to the large house, nestled on the hillside overlooking the fabulous bay of Hong Kong. It was a beautiful sight, especially at night, when the lights could be seen for miles around in a breathtaking view of a city that never seemed to sleep.

"I'm so glad you could come," the colonel told us as he met us at the door and led us into the bar. "Now, let me introduce you to my son and get you something to drink; then we can talk about Burma and India."

He told us many stories about his past military career. He had spent most of his adult life in Southeast Asia and said he simply couldn't ever go back to England. He wanted to stay where he was, even when his son was bound to return to England in a year or so.

"I've had every tropical disease there is," he added, which seemed like bragging in a way, although I couldn't imagine why anyone would brag about how many diseases he'd had, "and I have some of them still," he went on, "including dysentery, yellow fever, malaria, and"—he cleared his throat—"some others."

I didn't know what he meant by *some others*, or if he had made that throat-clearing noise to impress us or as a kind of warning. I let the waiter refill my drink a few times and was beginning not to care so much about what the colonel meant anymore.

We ate our dinner under colorful Chinese lanterns on the large veranda. As night fell, the lights came on all over the city and on the boats in the water. I felt as though I wanted to capture the sight forever.

I thought to myself, *If only Betty and the boys were here with me now*, while I sipped a cool rum punch decorated with thin slices of orange and lime, *everything would be absolutely perfect*.

I was getting a little bit tipsy, but that didn't matter to me. Then Sam announced it was time for us to go.

"Oh, don't go yet," the colonel said. "The evening is yet to begin! This is Hong Kong after all, the city of sexual freedom. Don't you just love all the women and boys who make themselves available here? I'm sure you have noticed them."

Then he snapped his fingers, and as Sam and I looked at each other, we both seemed to know what the other was thinking. I couldn't stop thinking about the diseases the colonel still had, and I wondered which ones might be catching, so I got ready to give my excuses to him and thank his son for their hospitality. I got up to leave for the hotel, but the colonel insisted that we stay, as he said, "We have a little surprise before you go." At this point, he clapped his hands, a signal at which five young girls and two boys appeared and stood in a line in front of Sam and me. The girls were wearing long, slinky see-through dresses, and their hair was long and black.

Sam's face had lost any expression that had been obvious just a moment earlier; all he did was stare wide-eyed straight ahead of him. I looked back at the colonel and his son. The old boy motioned with his arm, waving it out in front of him.

"Just pick yourself one or two, Sergeant," he offered. "They're yours for the night."

The son had already left the room with one of the girls and one boy. As I stood there, feeling my legs go all wobbly beneath me, Sam seemed to come to my rescue, saying, "Well, I'm not one to refuse a good piece of ass, Mark, but I think we both need to get back to the hotel right about now. What do you say, buddy?"

"Sure enough," I replied. "We'll find a taxi. Only five Hong Kong dollars. Okay, GI?"

"Okay, GI," Sam said, and we were gone.

# CHAPTER SIXTEEN

I DIDN'T GET INTO Saigon until I had to go to Tan Son Nhut Air Base to review some personnel records regarding a few of my airmen's upcoming promotions. I went with Danny Albany, another NCO, a real gung ho soldier who was just about twenty-two. Since there was no room for us to stay at the base, we checked into a downtown hotel. We decided to go out for a beer, and as soon as we walked in the door of the bar, we heard somebody shout out, "Give my Air Force buddy whatever he wants!"

Then he turned to us and said, "Come on over and sit with us."

He and his friend, both dressed in civilian clothes, looked all right to me. Ever since my days at San Quentin, I'd learned to size a man up pretty well, and whenever someone gave me the gut feeling that he wasn't okay, I just avoided him. I was usually right in my judgments. There was no gut feeling warning me to find a seat somewhere else, so Danny and I sat down and introduced ourselves.

Their names were John and Juan, which made me laugh when they said it. Juan started to speak with a Spanish accent. I picked up on it and responded in Spanish.

"Hey, I can't believe you speak Spanish," he responded in Spanish. "That's terrific!"

"It's my native tongue," I said. "My father was Basque. He taught us to speak in the Basque dialect when my brother and sisters and I were kids, but I haven't practiced speaking it in quite a while, so it's slipped away somewhat. Or maybe it's just that my Basque vocabulary belongs to a child, since I was so young when I stopped speaking it."

"That's funny," the Spaniard said, "but I think I know what you mean. I learned a little German when I was a kid, and now I dream in German sometimes, so I must remember it in some part of my brain. But when I'm awake, it disappears into thin air and I could hardly tell you my name in German."

He was a friendly guy, and I liked him right off. I don't know how long he and John had been drinking, so maybe it wasn't right of me to judge him when he wasn't sober, but as soon as I asked the question, "What's a Spaniard like you doing in this part of the world?" I wished that I had never joined this man and his friend for a drink. All his cheerfulness seemed to disappear into thin air, just like the guy had said about his memory of the German language.

He grew very silent, looking around over his shoulder to see who might be listening to him. We were seated at a corner table, so I guess he thought it was safe enough for him to speak without being spied on. Then he motioned for us to get our heads closer to him as he leaned over the table and whispered, "Have you ever heard of Operation Phoenix?" I started to speak. "Shh!" John said to me, turning around to see if anyone was listening. "Shut up soldier," he said bluntly. "This is a goddamn secret we're telling you! Understand?"

Sure, I understood; at least, it looked that way to me from the suspicious way they were acting.

Then Juan continued. "We work for the CIA, but we're not agents, see? There are only twelve of us—just like the Dirty Dozen. Our job is to locate villages under VC control. We wait until the men go out to find the enemy, and then we move in, killing every kid and woman and all the old people who are still left."

A shiver went up my spine, straight through me, and I wondered why, *if this were really true*, they were telling us about it. We were strangers to them, and might even have been CIA operatives ourselves, so he could have gotten himself into a lot of trouble by spilling the beans like this. As if his story wasn't bad enough, his buddy had to get his own story in.

"We burn everything that burns," John said. "The CIA pays us more money than we could make, hmm, say, anywhere, in ten years, so we come into Saigon every chance we get and blow most of it!"

I didn't know whether to buy these stories or not, but Danny was so impressed that his mouth was just about hanging open, and he kept on saying, "Wow! That's incredible!"

Being so much older, and I hope somewhat wiser than my young companion, I said, "So how did you guys ever get tangled up with the CIA?"

Juan took a long drink, finishing off the glass, and looking straight into my eyes, answered, "They came to me. I didn't go to them. The CIA looks all over Europe for guys like us. Don't they, John? We all have police records, so we're easy to find. We're murderers, you know. Killing people means nothing to us. Some of us are ex–Foreign Legionnaires. Soldiers of fortune. Mercenaries, if you will. It's as simple as that."

I'd seen the look in his ice-cold brown eyes before, many times, mostly at San Quentin but also when I was in Guam. They were the same eyes that I saw on the hangman's face.

I was beginning to feel a little uneasy, wishing I were someplace else, anywhere else, even back in Phan Rang. I stood up to leave and Danny gave me a look that seemed to ask if we really had to go. I said, "We have a plane to catch," even though we weren't going anywhere that night.

When the Spaniard stood to say good-bye, I couldn't help noticing his underarm holster and gun as well as the machete hanging from his belt.

For years after my encounter with those men, I looked for information about Operation Phoenix, asking innocent-sounding questions whenever I met someone who might have known about it. Everyone who had ever heard of it gave me the same response: those guys were nothing but cold-blooded killers, and Saigon was full of them at that time. Whenever they themselves got killed, the CIA could just give out a call for killers, like reaching into a pocket full of coins, and pull them out, bad pennies all of them.

It made me wonder what I was doing there, or for that matter, what all of us who wore the US uniform were doing there. As Danny and I ran into other groups of men that night, they were often friendly, willing to buy us a beer and draw us into conversation. They all had stories to tell, some of them hair-raising, rotten, and cruel. In my career, I had defended myself and my country against attack, but I'd never deliberately killed a man, and maybe I was lucky not to find myself in a kill-or-be-killed situation. Even so, I would never have offered up my services to any government for a price. I was just happy to get the hell out of Saigon, which seemed to me, especially that night, to be a city filled with sin and worse.

When the time came, I was happy to get the hell out of Vietnam, even though I had to practically die first to do it. I'd been away from Betty and the boys for about ten months when I woke up early one Sunday morning, and as I reached out to open the door, I felt as if someone had stuck a large needle right through me. The pain started in my back and worked its way straight across my gut. I doubled over, holding my stomach as if it were about to explode, and as I tried to straighten up, the pain got even worse.

It was hurting so badly that I yelled out for help, then yelled even louder, until some of the guys came in and rushed me to the infirmary with a bad case of kidney stones, as they later told me. I would have to be evacuated to the field hospital in Cam Rahn Bay. The next day I was loaded onto a C-130, although I hardly remember the trip since they'd injected me with very strong pain relievers.

I didn't really care what they did to me, since I'd never known pain like that before. Whenever it came, I felt as if it were tearing my insides right out. Since the medics couldn't keep pumping me with painkillers twenty-four hours a day, I had to live with the pain until my operation. But they'd have to medevac me to Clark Air Base in the Philippines.

Just as they were getting ready to take me out to the airfield and put me on a transport, I heard a telephone ring somewhere down the hall. The next minute, someone was calling out my name.

"Sergeant Vergara? Telephone call for Mark Vergara!"

A telephone call for me? Who in the world would be calling me on the phone, out in the middle of nowhere? It was so out of the ordinary that I couldn't believe it.

Some of the guys helped me, half carrying and half dragging my body to the phone. I had the receiver in my hand and brought it up to my ear; it felt like a completely foreign thing, as if I'd never even seen such a thing before. "Hello?" I asked, wondering if anyone was really on the other end or whether this was just some kind of a drug-related dream I was having.

Then I heard someone say, "It's me, Betty!" but I didn't know what to do about it for the longest time.

*Betty?* I thought. *That's my wife's name! It couldn't possibly be my Betty. Could it?*

"Mark, it's me," she said. "Can you hear me? Are you all right? Oh, darling, are you okay? What are you doing in the hospital?"

Then everything seemed to click, and I knew exactly what to do with the phone, and what to say. I was talking a mile a minute suddenly, as if someone had set my fuse and it was burning straight up along my arteries, from my toes to the tip of my head!

"How in the world did you know where to find me?" I asked, after explaining that I was sick and waiting to be flown to the hospital.

"Well, I knew you were sick, darling, because I've been trying to find you all over Vietnam, and it's taken me practically all night. Thank God they finally located you for me, and I caught you in time to say hello and good-bye. Mark, dear, are you all right? And are they taking good care of you?"

"Maybe I should have gotten sick sooner, huh?" I answered. But then the guys were pulling at my sleeve to let me know the plane was going to take off without me if I didn't get the hell off the phone. I said good-bye, telling Betty exactly where they were taking me, and she promised to call every other day while I was in the Philippines.

When we got to the hospital at Clark Air Base, I was given a blue-dye injection for an X-ray, and apparently I was allergic to it and went into a coma for days. No one knew if I'd pull out of it or not. I don't remember much about it myself, except that I seemed to be dreaming half the time and felt as if someone or something was pulling me down, way down into the lower depths of an underground place with a hundred tunnels leading nowhere and no exits and nowhere to sit and rest. All I could see was a light, far away at the end of the tunnels, but I could never reach it.

I was tired, like someone who had been running for days, months, or years. I was so tired, my legs felt as heavy as lead. I could hardly move my legs at all and seemed to lose control of my muscles completely, so that I wouldn't have known how to walk if I'd been strong enough to stand up.

"I'll help you, Dad," someone was saying to me. "I'm strong enough now to help you. Big enough to join the Army too," said the voice. Somewhere in the back of my mind, I realized that it was my son Mark Jr. "If you did it, Dad, I can do it too."

I didn't know if I was on the phone or drifting out into outer space or just dreaming that I was dreaming. It was all so unreal that I couldn't get a handle on it. I tried to separate out what must have been my conscious, actual conversations with my kids on the phone and distinguish them from fantasies I must have been having in the drugged semiconsciousness of my postoperative state.

I was living in that hazy twilight zone for weeks. It was only during my last few days of recuperating that I realized I was being shipped back home, right back to March Air Force Base in Riverside, California, where I had been stationed years before.

I didn't find out for sure about Mark Jr. until I finally saw him standing next to his mother with Dorothy and my granddaughter on one side of Betty and our Jeremy on the other, all running up to me as I walked off the plane, throwing their arms around me in a family bear hug. I had to fight hard to keep the tears back in my eyes, where they belonged, because I didn't want anyone to see me crying on my return from Vietnam. I'd just come back from hell, and men don't cry, even when they find themselves back, by some miracle, in heaven again.

Before I had even dropped my duffel bag on the ground or moved a step from the spot we were all standing, still huddled together like some half-baked football team, I shook my head and said, "This is it, folks. I've had it with the service, and I'm quitting! Tomorrow or even today, right this minute! Take me to the nearest phone, because I know I'm never going back to 'Nam again, and I know I'm never going to leave my family again either." That was when Mark Jr. dropped his bomb on me.

"I've signed up with the paratroopers, Dad," he said.

Then we all broke out of the circle and stood, staring at him, nodding and sighing as if we were at a funeral and didn't know what to say to the surviving members of the grieving family.

"Let's go home and talk about it, son," I quietly said, wrapping my arm across his shoulders as we started walking toward the car. "I have so much I'd like to tell you before you make up your mind."

"We can still have a talk," he told me, "but I'm afraid my mind is already made up."

"I'm afraid too, Mark," I said, "and that's just what I want to talk to you about."

# CHAPTER SEVENTEEN

"NOTHING IS GOING to stop me, Dad," Mark Jr. was saying as we all sat around the breakfast table the next morning. He was drinking coffee now, and although it surprised me to see how very grown up he had become, I didn't let him know how deeply troubled and unhappy his decision had made me. I just listened to him with a straight face, and the room was so quiet during the lulls in our conversation that I could hear my wife's breathing as she stood at the kitchen window staring out.

She had apparently had the same conversation with Mark, knowing all his reasons for signing up and not really wanting to hear them again. I think the only reason she stayed in the kitchen with us was to pick up the pieces if either of us should break down.

"Anyway, if you look at it from my point of view," he went on, lighting a cigarette and blowing out the match, "I'm just following your footsteps, Dad. So how can you say no when I want to do the exact same thing that you've been doing all your life?"

He was right. I had been in the military most of my life, and I loved it and would have probably stayed in the Air Force if there hadn't been any Vietnam.

"I can't say no," I told Mark. "And besides, I don't think you're asking for my permission. Are you, Mark?"

"No, sir, I'm not."

It was funny, the way he kept calling me *sir*. It was a word he'd have to use a lot in the Army, but he seemed so young to be speaking to me in such a formal way. In the year since I'd been gone, I'd thought of him as a boy. I had even put up some old photos of the two boys and Dorothy when they were children, taken on our vacation in Ensenada. I'd been looking at their photos every day and must have deluded myself into thinking they were still as young as the kids in those snapshots. Deluded myself into believing that time had been standing still while I was away, as if I'd find them unchanged when I got back.

I wanted my two boys to be young again, to jump up into my lap and hug me as they did when they were little. I wanted Mark to say, Aw, I'm only fooling, Daddy. I just wanted to play soldier with the other guys, that's all. I'd much rather be a banker or even a farmer when I grow up!

But he wasn't a child anymore. He was, by anyone's definition of the word, a man, and man enough to make up his own mind about his own future. He was trying to tell me how important it was for him to join up, as if I needed to be persuaded what a wonderful life he could have in the Army.

"Listen, son, I know that nothing I say now will change your mind," I said, "but I do want you to go over there with your eyes wide open, so I should tell you that . . ."

I wanted to tell him that I would never have volunteered to go to 'Nam. When I joined way back in 1942, the world had been a different place altogether, and we ended up fighting a different kind of war. In Vietnam, he would be fighting against enemies he could hardly see and wouldn't necessarily recognize if they walked right up to him on the street and shook his hand because they looked the same as the people he'd be trying to protect.

I wanted to tell him there was no hope of ever winning this war, since the only way to win in Vietnam was to blow the country all to hell.

So why go and fight a war that can't be won? I wanted to say. I knew it was too late to say anything, since he would be leaving for Fort Ord to be processed in a few days.

Betty was standing with her back to us, and she began to wash the dishes in the sink, but I could tell from the trembling in her shoulders that she was crying. She had only turned the water on to hide the sound of her sorrow.

I felt as if my fatherhood was over, and I felt cheated because I'd missed so much of my boys' growing-up years. Now, in Mark's youthful manhood, he was leaving of his own accord, and there was nothing I could say or do to stop him. I could have told him some of the horror stories of 'Nam, but my hands were tied since there was no longer a question of whether Mark was going or not. As far as he was concerned, he was already gone, so I handed in my resignation with a mixture of joy and sadness, because for me, my career had finally come to an end, just as my son's was starting.

After twenty-four years of active service, I applied for retirement, and with Betty at my side, on August 1, 1967, the base commander at Travis Air Force Base shook my hand and said, "Thanks for your many years of active duty and your devotion to your country. We are proud of men like you, Sergeant."

And that, as they say, was that. There were no parades, no dinners, no fanfare. Just a handshake from a commander I didn't even know. And yet, the time was right for me to leave the service, just as it was right for Mark Jr. to enter it. We decided to have a joint celebration by going out for a fancy dinner. Even as we toasted one another with numerous glasses of champagne, I couldn't help thinking that soon, very soon, we'd be separated once again.

I wasn't sure that he would ever come back. I'd been unsure of my own future, and I hadn't been on many dangerous missions. But Mark wanted to fight, as Jeremy told me one afternoon, reminding me of the talks I used to have with the first Jeremy I knew, whose name I had given to my son.

Sitting on the edge of his bed, Jeremy was reading a book. The door to his room was open, so I asked whether it was all right for me to join him.

"Sure, Dad. Do want to talk about Mark?"

I tousled his hair with my hand and said, "You're a pretty smart kid, for being the youngest in the family!"

"Sometimes it helps, being the younger son, 'cause your brother can go ahead and try things out for the first time, and then you know what to do and what not to do!"

"How do you feel about Mark's enlistment?"

He closed the book and put it on his lap, then looked at me as if he were the older one. He answered me the way a father might answer his own son. "It's his life, Dad. If he wants to go, we can't stop him. I only hope he comes back, like you did. I don't want to be the surviving son."

I knew that Jeremy and Mark had always been a little jealous of each other; after all, they were brothers, always competing with each other. I never knew until then how really close they actually were. I was filled with pride for my two sons. They were both strong and smart, standing tall in their young manhood. They were now two men I was very proud of. They both had strong feelings for each other, a typical Basque trait. They were my sons. Sons of a Basque.

"You know what, young man?" I asked Jeremy, putting my arm around his back. "I'm sure glad you're staying home to keep me company while Mark is overseas. I'll be depending on you to keep a stiff upper lip for the next year or so, son, to be a good influence on your mom."

"Thanks, Dad, I will be," he answered, opening his book again and finding the place where he'd left off. I knew he would have said more, but he was a bit embarrassed by my show of affection, at least I thought so. I got up and quietly closed the door behind me, happy I'd had the chat with him.

Mark Jr. was eventually sent to Fort Benning, Georgia, for boot camp, and then assigned to the Ninth Infantry in Vietnam, in a part of that country known as the Delta, an area with nothing but swamp grass growing higher than a man's head, which was the perfect setup for VC ambushes.

He was the point man in his squad on search-and-destroy missions, spending days going through the rice paddies, sleeping on dikes, soaking wet. It took him years to open up a bit and tell me about some of his experiences. He wasn't ashamed to tell me that he'd cried like a little kid when his buddy fell dead at his side. I wasn't ashamed to hear him say it, since I knew what he must have been feeling, sitting in the rice paddy while the world seemed to be blowing up right before his eyes.

I became like an expectant father all over again, staying up with Betty almost every night and pacing the floor when I couldn't sleep. Sometimes I would even wake up in the middle of a nightmare, with the sweat pouring off my forehead and neck as if someone had emptied a bucket of water over me during the night.

Betty had started talking in her sleep, mumbling the craziest things, mostly about Mark, naturally. One night she started hitting me, even as she slept, hitting my chest and arms and saying, "No, don't! Stop hurting him! Leave him alone!"

When he went to 'Nam, Mark had a head of brown hair, even though there wasn't much of it left after the barber got through with him. When he came back from the Delta a year later, what was left of his hair was almost white. I was proud of Mark for having made his decision and sticking to it and for living long enough to come back to us, by the grace of God.

Nothing will ever be able to bring back the lives of the men who died there, but hopefully, men like my son will remember it well enough to warn their children, and maybe they will be brave enough, as men, to say, "No more war for us, not ever again."

All of us want to make our mark in the world, even if it's just to say, "I was here," or "I passed through this place on my way to somewhere else." The expression in Spanish would be *Pasó por aquí*. I guess it has exactly the same meaning as the little drawing that the soldiers used to leave all over Europe during the First World War that showed the top of a man's head, his hands, and the tip of his nose peeping over a fence with the caption "*Kilroy was here.*"

Sometimes it's enough to leave a physical sign of our presence, such as our initials chiseled into a tree trunk or on a wooden tabletop. Sometimes we try to do it by having children to pass on our family name and keep the family lines going on through generations. And some of us are so moved by our life experiences that we are driven by some inner need to write them down, leaving our words for future generations to read and thereby know us.

And so, as the son of a Basque, with this book, I pass down the story of my life for my children and their children to read, knowing full well that they, too, will find some way to leave their mark in the world, as the grandsons and granddaughters of the first Basque generations who found their own unique way of saying *Pasó por aquí*.

# EPILOGUE

MY DAD PASSED in 1998, just one year after I moved to Florida. He was suffering from Parkinson's and a touch of dementia when I left California, but he surprised me by saying "Watch out for alligators." That was the last time I saw him alive.

My mother moved to Florida a couple of years after his death. I was able to see her often; however, she never made reference to the book Dad had been working on. But when my mother fell ill in 2017 with lung cancer, it wasn't surprising for us to find out that she had saved everything.

After Mom's passing, my daughter Deborah and I were going through her things, trying to find something in remembrance of her and my dad. We came across a huge storage box filled to the top with papers. Not knowing what exactly it was, Deb placed it in my car along with other things and told me to take it home.

When I opened the storage box, I found my dad's manuscript. It was interspersed with clippings and notes—my mom never threw anything away. I began going through it and contacted Deb, asking if we should try to get the book published.

Deb asked me to send the material to her, and between the two of us, we began to put the pieces together. It was quite amazing how everything fell into perfectly good order. It brings tears to my eyes just remembering how it all came about.

I have read the book a few times now, and each time I do, I want to cry and smile at the same time. My dad: what a life! He is a hero in my eyes, and I thank God he was able to write his memoir—things he never spoke about while I was growing up. And what a story he had to tell.

There's so much to be proud of. My brothers and I are truly in awe.

We buried my mother in the same place as my father. They were a team, she being a Brit and my dad a Basque.

Dorothy Stangle

# ABOUT THE AUTHOR

**MARK B. ARRIETA** was born in Delta, Colorado, in 1918 and was the oldest child of Mary and Miguel Arrieta, Basque and Mexican/Native American immigrants. His father had been a famous bullfighter in the Basque Country of northern Spain, but after being gored by a bull, his fragile health kept the family poor and often hungry. Mark lost his father at the age of ten, and he was thrust into the role of breadwinner and head of the family.

Throughout his childhood and adolescence, he worked in the beet fields of Colorado before and after school, alongside his six younger siblings and his mother. Destitute and forced to move into an inhospitable, crime-ridden boarding house, Mark learned how to fight and stand up for himself.

At the age of sixteen, after paying off the family's old debts, he jumped a freight train and headed to the golden state of California, where he hoped to build a better life. His first job there was working for the Civilian Conservation Corps, but when World War II broke out in Europe, he enlisted in the Army Air Corps and soon began the life of a military man. From the Pacific to the European Theater, Mark flew in B-17s as a tail gunner. He survived twenty-five missions but saw his entire flight crew shot down as he helplessly lay in the infirmary. The guilt of surviving his best friend, Jeremy, stayed with him his whole life. The emotional scars and physical injuries he suffered were burdens that he carried going forward.

For a short time, he worked as a prison guard at one of the country's deadliest prisons, San Quentin, where he witnessed daily acts of violence and cruelty. Because of this experience, he was hired to serve as prison supervisor at the Army Air Corps stockade in Guam. He also served as an Air Force recruiter in Torrance, California, and Moses Lake, Washington. His favorite military post was being stationed in England for four years in the late 1950s.

His last military assignment was in Vietnam, where he was in charge of security for a new airstrip being built. During his eighteen months there, he had numerous near-death encounters with stealthy tigers, deadly cobras, and armed Viet Cong villagers.

Throughout it all, he maintained his wits, integrity, and commitment by remembering that the sacrifices he was making were for the good of his family: his wife, Betty May Forbes, whom he met in England during the war, and his three children, Dorothy, Mark Jr., and Jeffrey. Together, they were his beacon home and gave him a sense of purpose.

After leaving the military, Mark quietly began the life of a civilian as the owner of a doughnut shop. And when the military came knocking on his door again, offering him an exorbitant sum of money to work as a spy in Cuba, he firmly turned them down.

Mark lived until the age of seventy-nine. From his hardship and poverty in early life to his wartime battles and the victories he experienced in the military, he was happiest telling the tales from the comfort of his well-worn armchair with his children and grandchildren around him.

He wrote this book as a tribute to the father he barely knew—the proud Basque bullfighter.

**DEBORAH DRIGGS** is the granddaughter of Mark B. Arrieta. Known for her acting roles in *Night Rhythms*, *Total Exposure*, and *Neon Bleed*, she has also been a *Playboy* centerfold and cover girl, a member of the Screen Actors Guild, and a top-rated insurance industry professional. Deborah has overcome a number of challenges by being willing to take risks and maintain a positive attitude.

Pursuing her interest in dance, Deborah won a spot on the US Football League cheerleading squad and joined a professional dance company touring Japan. When she returned to Los Angeles, she began her modeling career and auditioned for *Playboy*. After posing as a centerfold, she was invited to grace the cover of the March and April 1990 issues of *Playboy*—the leading men's magazine in the world at the time—which led to opportunities as a VJ (video jockey) for the Playboy Channel's *Hot Rocks* show and appearances in several rock videos.

Dedicated to helping women break through negative self-talk and take on any challenge, Deborah—who is on a healing path herself— knows the difference it can make to have a helping hand when one needs it the most. Her response to internal struggles is "If there is a struggle, then there is a problem, and in that problem there is a beautiful, simple solution for complicated souls!"

To contact Deborah, visit www.deborahdriggs.com or email her at deborah@deborahdriggs.com.